RIHANI
The Darkness
by
M.Rigoni

Illustrations by Benito M. Brancalion
Cover by Sandra Nooke

Although the characters within this book are fictional and do not specifically relate to any one culture, the story is intertwined with anthropological information, beliefs and legends from the people who still inhabit the islands of the Pacific.

First published 2015 by Marmolada Pty Ltd
Copyright © Maria Rigoni 2015
The moral right of the author has been asserted.
ISBN: 978-0-9873544-1-9

In memory of my loving mother

Contents

Illustrations

By Sandra Noke
Front Cover

By Benito Mario Brancalion
Prologue. 19th century whaling ship. Based on rendering of 'The Essex' 1815
Chapter 2. Volcano Island Central Pacific
Chapter 8. Trading ships
Chapter 11.Old ship hulk used as prisons. Based on wood engraving of convict hulk found in State Library of Victoria
Chapter 16. Mother Hubbard dress
Chapter 19. Tamed noddy birds in front of huts
Chapter 22. Empty coconut shells used to carry water
Chapter 24. The white tern
Epilogue. Shell armband based on Kula armband

Acknowledgements

I would like to thank the following people for making this book possible.
To the people of the Pacific Islands whose stories, history, myths and legends are the essence of this book.
Sandra for the wonderful cover.
Caitlilin who proofread and edited the manuscript.
Don who endlessly discussed the characters and made valued suggestions and insights into human behaviour.
My siblings and their families John, Miriam, Johnny, Giulia, Anthony, Sharon for always being there for me.
My wonderful sons and their wives Adrian, Penny, Denis, TuQuan, for their constant support and love and for giving me my beautiful grandchildren, Kiara, Aiden, Raquel, Dante, Poppy.
A special thanks to TuQuan who first edited and made valued recommendations to the original manuscript.
Adrian without his help I would not have been able to publish this book.
My husband Mario whose illustrations added meaning and beauty to the story.

Thank you

Prologue

Whaling ship 19th century.

In the nineteenth century, hundreds of ships sailed throughout the Pacific Ocean hunting whales. The overpopulated cities throughout Europe and America were in great need of oil to fuel lamps and make soap, perfume and other materials from whale blubber and bones. These increasing demands led to new innovations such as brick ovens, called the 'tryworks', which were installed on ships. With these, whalers could process the whale parts into oil and fat and then these stored in barrels. This processing at sea allowed ships to travel further and further into uncharted oceans. Voyages would often last for many years and on these hazardous journeys, new lands were discovered.   Ships would often need to stop at many of the unmapped islands. On some islands, the natives were friendly and would gladly trade food and water for beads, mirrors, hatchets, knives and guns. However, on other islands, crew members were killed and sometimes eaten by cannibals.

The Polynesians and Micronesians had lived on tiny, remote volcanic islands for hundreds and hundreds of years. Stories of where their ancestors came from and their journeys across thousands of miles of ocean in fragile outrigger canoes were forgotten, and only some of the myths, ancient beliefs and customs survived. Progress for the people on these isolated islands was very slow. They relied on their beliefs and the resources that surrounded them to survive.

Contact with the 'white man' was devastating for most of these traditional societies. It tore at their very survival, and in many cases it was the end of their culture. Belief systems that were the very core of their existence crumbled, leaving social upheaval and the loss of their unique identities forever.

Chapter One

Avery Jones

Avery kept his eyes closed against the bright light that blinded him. His skin was so badly burnt by the sun that his body was covered with festering ulcers and sores. He could do nothing but lay lifeless on top of his precarious raft that was part of the wreckage of what remained of the whaleboat.

*   *   *   *

London 1805

"Whot you got?" asked Will, one of the two firemen on duty.

"It's a wee mite," replied Jones.

Will walked across to Jones who had picked up a small baby wrapped in a dirty bloody rag.

"It dead?"

"Not far off. Tha cord 'as been cut, but it's still got blood ova it."

"Whot ye gonna do wit it?"

"Take it to tha orphanage on Queen Street, I suppose. It'll probably die, but what else is there to do. Whot you think?"

"Hasn't much chance, it's nearly dead. Better just leave it and we'll dig a hole out back."

"We gotta give it a chance. I'm taking it to Queen Street."

Jones held his small, bloodied bundle to his chest and quickly walked to the orphanage. He knew the baby had little hope of survival. Many babies died, but this one had to be given a chance. "Not that being alive is that great, mite. Maybe it's betta you die," mumbled Jones to the small, listless body.

Mrs Alders walked to the front door as Jones knocked for the third time. "Comin'! Comin'!" she yelled impatiently.

Mrs Alders was a small, plump, middle-aged woman with grey hair pulled tightly into a severe chignon on the back of her head. She wore a grubby apron on top of a black muslin dress. Mrs Alders had worked at the orphanage for most of her life. She did not have any children of her own for Mr Alders had died at sea just after they had married.

At first she felt pity for the unwanted babies who were brought to the orphanage. But as time went by, she had become more and more indifferent. Too many of the babies died, so she no longer became attached to them. She did what was expected of her and then the fate of the babies was left in God's hands.

Jones held out the dirty bundle and Mrs Alder sighed. "Another one! Can't keep taking more. Where do I put 'im? Gotta get your name before you go, has to be in the book," she continued.

"Jones. Me name's Jones. Found the mite down the station. Is it a boy, then?" But he turned and headed back to the station without waiting for a reply.

Mrs Alder took the baby and said to the maid, "Gilly, get this babe. It'll probably die, but see if it will take some milk.

Warm, but not too hot either." With this. Mrs Alder

handed over the dirty bundle and turned to leave.

"Whot we called it? Is it a boy?" asked Gilly.

"The man who found him was named Jones. So I suppose we could call him Jones. You pick a first name. I ran out of names."

"I like Avery. Sounds special, don't it?" stated Gilly as she unwrapped the baby and saw that it was indeed a boy.

"Sounds like a nob's name if ye ask me," shrugged Mrs Alders.

"He may become a hoity-toity nob if'n 'e lives," Gilly replied enthusiastically.

"Then so it be. His name's Avery Jones. Now I gotta go write 'im in the book," Mrs Alder sighed wearily.

Gilly took the baby and cradled it in one arm. The tiny child was still bloodied from its birth, but Gilly would not wash him until he drank some of the milk first. With her free hand, she put some warm milk into a bottle with a teat and tried to feed it to the infant.

At first the baby ignored the teat, still too cold and weak from its ordeal. But then, with some insistence from Gilly, it slowly attempted to suck it.

Gilly knew that the milk had been watered down and at times it was off. Wet nurses were hard to find and there were already too many babies in the orphanage.

Unless another small child died, little Avery would have to be contented with watered-down animal milk.

Once the baby had sucked a little of the warm milk, Gilly unfolded the dirty rags that covered him, and with a wet rag she washed the dry blood from his tiny body. She then swaddled him in clean cloths and carried him up to the already full nursery.

It was very quiet for a room full of babies, but they had soon learned to give up their crying, for nobody came to comfort them when they did.

Avery was placed in a cot next to another two small bodies.

Gilly looked at him and sighed. "I hope you live, little Avery Jones."

Avery Jones did survive and spent the first years of his life in the orphanage. Like many children in the orphanage, no one ever claimed or adopted him.

Still, he had been one of the lucky ones to survive the first years of his life, as many of the other small children had died. When he was four, he was sent to a workhouse as a 'pauper apprentice'.

He received only board and lodgings, and worked from before sunrise until late at night. Avery had been badly beaten on numerous occasions. There never seemed to be any real reason for it, except that his masters seemed to take delight in humiliation and pain.

Avery knew he could not escape from the factory, because if he were recaptured he would be whipped and shackled. He had witnessed what happened to some of the other boys who had tried to escape from their masters.

They were treated even worse when they were returned. Besides, where would he go?

The sum of Avery's life was written on his back.

The crisscross of scars from the numerous beating and

whippings related to each new master from the orphanage to the whaling ship the Planter. He had been sold from one owner to another, and each time his master was crueller than before and expected more from him.

His harsh life and lack of food meant Avery was very small for his age, so people were never quite sure how old he was.

It had been his master at the tannery who had sold him to the whaling ship. "Ye ain't worth much, but I'll take whot I can get. Lots more free boys at the orphanage," the old man had sniggered.

At first Avery thought he had finally left his life of misery and pain for great adventures. On the whaling ship he would not only have food and lodgings, but his contract also gave him a 'lay-wage', which was a small share of the take, to be distributed at the end of the voyage.

Avery's clothes and other expenses would be deducted from his share. Avery was excited, as he had never before received any money for the work he had done.

He quickly found that life on board the ship was little better than in the factories where he had worked.

His labours were dangerous and dirty. At about 14 years of age, he was the youngest member of the crew and assigned the role of the cabin boy. Ostensibly his job was to sweep the deck and coil any stray ropes that were left lying about.

However, in reality his job consisted of doing all the dirtiest work that the other crew members were reluctant to do.

"Getta scrubbin' the deck, then clean the fat spilt on

the tryworks when yer done!" would be the constant shout from one of the crew, but before he could finish these chores, another crew member would yell yet more orders.

"The cook needs yer, so getta move on!" He could never rest from the moment he woke until late into the night.

Avery was also expected to be aboard one of the boats that were lowered from the ship to harpoon the whales. He was not afraid to do this. In fact, it was the only time he felt excited to be on board the whaling ship.

There were three whaleboats on board the Planter, with six oarsmen and an officer stationed in each boat

The cook, the steward and the cooper, who made and repaired the casks – were left on board as 'shipkeepers'. It was their job to look after the ship whilst the other crew members were chasing the whales.

The crew also kept watch in four hour-long shifts, and Avery too was expected to do this. At times, however, his shift would entail more than four hours, as some of the crew would threatened him and he had to take their shift as well.

"Reckon yer young, so you don't have-ta rest as much as us, 'cause we work more," the crew members would say, and Avery did not have the courage to refuse them, for he would get beaten if he did.

The crew's quarters were called the 'forcastle', which was a triangular shaped room with narrow bunks lining the walls. The men's sea chest, soap-kegs, greasy pans and tainted meat, as well as the crew themselves, all inhabited this dark, foul smelling, rat infested, smoky room below deck. The captain's and mate's cabins were at the back of the ship where the air was much cleaner.

The temperature below deck was so hot that often the stench within the cabin made Avery gag. He rarely slept in his bunk, preferring to find a secluded spot upside. Each night he tried to find a different place.

He was afraid of the comments and taunts whispered about him by some of the crew. At night, when he was allowed to rest, he would hide in fear.

Punishment on board was severe. If any member of the crew disobeyed orders, they would be put in irons or flogged with a whip comprised of nine knotted lines called a cat-o'-nine tails.

On the ship, the captain was the ultimate law and his orders had to be followed. Avery lived in fear of disobeying any member of the crew, for they were all bigger, rougher and crueller than him. Even so, Avery felt the cat-o'-nine tails many times.

When a crew member stole gin or extra food, Avery would be made to confess. The culprits would threaten to kill him if he did not take the blame and Avery knew that these were no idle threats.

On July 11, 1819, two of the crew looked up at the sky and stood paralysed in terror. High above, they saw a tail of falling fire. Samuel, one of the two men on watch that night, ran down to the captain's cabin. He knew he should not disturb the captain, for he was drunk most nights, but this was urgent.

"Captain! Captain! Captain!" yelled Samuel.
The captain finally awoke, cursing and staggered to the door in a foul mood. "WHAT'S UP?" he shouted.

"C-Captain, i-in da sky. Come look. It's a bad sign!"

The captain, grumbling, walked unsteadily up on deck and stood gazing at the night sky. He knew the men on board were superstitious, and he himself, although the captain, was also superstitious.

"It's a comet, you bunch of fools! It may mean we will have a good catch. Perhaps a large sperm whale," he sniggered.

The whalers preferred to hunt the sperm whale, for they were the most lucrative of the whale species.

The superior quality of the sperm whale oil made an exceptionally fine lubricant, and the ambergris was the basis of costly perfume. But although the sperm whale was the most sought after species, it was also the most dangerous to hunt.

The next day, the men were very quiet and sombre as they went about their duties on board. They all knew about the sign, so each in his own way was praying. Even those who were not religious seemed to develop faith and pray silently.

Three days after the comet was first sighted, the sun was shining and there was only a slight breeze. The blue expanse of sea seemed endless and peaceful.

"SPOUTS AHEAD!" yelled the lookout from the crow's nest.

The men all looked at the sea ahead of their ship. About a half a mile off, they could see the spout from a whale.

"LOWER THE BOATS!" shouted the captain.

Three boats were lowered, each manned by six crew members. The boats would row towards the spout and wait until they could see the dark shadow under the water surface.

Then they would hurl their harpoons at the whale, forcing it to surface. The other boats would come near and also launched their harpoons.

On this occasion, they missed and pulled the harpoons back to throw again, but before they could be launched, the whale turned and tail smashed the nearest boat with its tail, tipping the crew into the sea.

The frightened whale started swimming away, pulling with it the boat that had harpooned it. A crew member threw the storm drogue into the sea at the rear of the boat.

This acted as a type of parachute to slow the boat down and keep the hull perpendicular. The captain let the rope that was tied to the harpoon unwind as the whale picked up speed.

The men then braced themselves, for when the rope had reached its end there would be a sharp jerk and the whale would continue to pull the boat until it tired. The whale might swim for miles.

The other boat with the crew who had been thrown overboard headed back to the Planter. Once they were on board, the first mate yelled,

"Put the hard help up. We have to follow the captain." He then took out his spyglass and watched the whaleboat being pulled further and further away by the sperm whale.

The captain and crew who were on it kept clutching the sides of the boat. Avery was towards the back and was watching, mesmerised, as the gigantic whale pulled them further away from the ship.

Then it happened. The whale turned around and charged back at them. The men were horrified and unable to move, for there was nowhere for them to go.

The angry whale was coming straight at them, its jaws open wide. There was a tremendous crash and Avery found himself hurled up into the air before plunging down into the cold water with a loud splash.

He saw the grey-blue water around him as he sank under. He could not stop his fall and he descended further and further down into its depth. To Avery, it felt as if everything was happening in slow motion.

The sea around him became deathly quiet as he looked, fascinated, at the bubbles of air that escaped from his body. He started kicking his feet in an effort to swim back up to the surface.

He felt as if his lungs were exploding and wanted to open his mouth, but he knew that if he did he so would die. Instead, he started slowly letting out the air in his lungs. When he hit the surface, he gasped for air. Around him, the noise was thunderous.

Waves were crashing and frantic, choking yells could be heard everywhere. The dark, fearsome shape was still flicking its tail and smashing what remained of their boat.

The men could not swim away as the waves the whale was creating surrounded them and sucked them down into the vortex of dark churning water. Avery suddenly felt a sharp pain. Something hit his back and he began to sink underwater again. This time his downward plunge stopped closer to the surface.

Again he kicked as hard as he could and soared up

back to the surface. When he reached it, he spat out the water that filled his mouth and gasped for air.

In the midst of all the heaving, he glimpsed something floating nearby and realised it was part of the wreckage. He threw himself towards it as hard as he could.

He felt a hard surface and clung to it. He held on to it with all his might as the waves swept the wreckage further and further away from the angry whale. With his last remaining strength, he managed to pull himself onto the top of the makeshift raft. Exhausted, he collapsed.

Avery floated in and out of consciousness. When he surfaced from the dark corner of his mind, he was delirious. At times his body was shivering from the intense cold he felt.

He thought he was still in the orphanage, hungry and cold, his hands and feet swollen and sore from chilblains. At other times, he was hot and could feel perspiration trickling down his face into his burning eyes.

Then he believed he was still working in the fetid factory and could smell the putrid skins as he scraped fly invested flesh from the skins as he prepared them for tanning.

Little did Avery realise that the putrid smell was coming from his own body, for his wounds were slowly turning into seeping ulcers.

Once more, Avery felt the sharp lash across his back and screamed out in pain. "Get up you lousy good for nothin scum!" screamed a high-pitched voice as the leather strap cut in again, this time into his face. He could feel the lashes burning his flesh and tried desperately to get up, but he could not move. His body was paralysed.

The voice echoed into the distance, but the agonising pain was still present. Then the merciful cool dark space embraced him again. When he awoke, it was dark.

His body was in pain and the salty sea spray burnt his flesh. He could feel a deep cut on his leg, still sticky with blood.

His back must have also been hurt, because it too was very painful. Even if he could have moved, the raft was barely large enough to contain his body. So he just lay there, letting the darkness shroud his mind and take him to his cool, dreamless cocoon.

When he awoke again, he tried to look around. He was barely able to fit on the raft. It floated, but higher waves splashed over the edges. The wounds on his body were excruciating.

The sea salt stung his skin and his back ached. His throat felt as if he had swallowed a red hot coal. He tried to swallow to see if a little saliva would help, but his mouth was too parched and the exercise only worsened the pain.

He lay still and tried to will himself to escape into the cool corner of his mind where there was only oblivion. For how long he remained on the raft, he could not tell. Days merged into nights.

One dark night, he felt rain. At first it was cool and he opened his mouth to let the precious drops enter. But as the night continued, so did the rain and soon he felt cold. The rain had burst the blisters on his body and now they were, if possible, even more painful.

When he awoke again, he could hear a ringing in the distance. "It's the bells from the cathedral," he thought. He had often heard them and had sometimes walked passed the large ornate doors of the church.

People would enter there to pray to God, but Avery himself had never been taught how to do it. "How do I pray? And what would I pray for? I don't want to be rescued. I only want the pain to stop and to die.

People think I'm stupid because I don't speak to no one. Every day I only want to survive that day. Life is too hard!" he thought in despair.

He tried to open his eyes, but could only manage to let a sliver of light come through. He could make out a large black shadow, circling above him. The monstrous shadow had large black wings. Avery had heard of monsters that lived out here on the sea.

"Now it will come down and eat me alive," he sobbed, but no tears came to bathe and soothe his eyes. Thankfully, he returned again to his cool, dark cocoon.

Chapter Two
Rihani

Volcanic Island. Central Pacific.

The villagers sat patiently around the large fire on the reef. The fire was never for warmth, but it had always been part of the custom on the island. There was a hush as they waited for the old woman to begin. Only the gentle crashing of waves on the reef and a light breeze whispering in the high coconut trees could be heard. The old woman sat cross-legged on a worn pigskin mat. Her eyes were closed and her face showed signs of the passing of time. Her thin bony hands lay passively on her knees. She was a small woman and the passing years had shrivelled her body until resembled the old, gnarled trees high up on the mountain. Even at her unknown age, her skin was still darker than the other members of the tribe. Her fine, straggly, long, white hair hung over her bony shoulders. The old woman told her stories in a rhythmic, monosyllabic chant. The people of the tribe loved listening to the mysterious sound of her voice. It soothed them, for it sounded like the whispering wind and gentle waves that caressed their shore. She began to speak.

"In the beginning of time, our people lived beneath the earth. They lived as we do, in clans, classes and villages. They owned land and coconut trees and were versed in magic. Then one day, the people climbed up to the surface through holes. First came a tortoise that also lived underground and it became the totem of our clan. In other holes on our island, different animals appeared. There was the eel for the U'ulu clan, the octopus for the Deibi clan, the reef shark for the Iwa clan, the tree lizard for the Kalab clan, and the crab for the Yarle clan. Then from these holes emerged the first sister and brother, followed by the rest of the people. These were our first ancestors and they brought with them the knowledge of how to do things, our traditions and magic. Our clan emerged through the sacred pinnacle. In the pool beneath the pinnacle, the water has magic powers that help us when we are sick. And when we die our spirits must pass through the gap at the top of the sacred rock.

At first, we lived together in peace. We were all one, living together. We wore no rini. Our bodies were painted with the colour of our earth and our hair was white. The sea was always full of fish and the birds were plentiful. We ate only raw meat and raw fish because the gods had not given us the gift of the sacred fire. At night, the people moved to the sound of drums. All the girls were big with babies.

Our clan had great wealth and power. Many of the other clans were jealous and so the killing started. For many years our people died in those long wars: men, women and children. It was our great sorceress Ekewane, risking her own life, who stood between the warring tribes and called upon our ancestors to stop the killing. Ekewane married her friend Emarr. He had rescued her after she had been kidnapped and was being forced to marry loopu, chief Ramanmada's unstable son. Over time Emarr became a great chief…"

Rihani sat gazing into the flickering flames, listening to the old woman's words. Rihani was very beautiful and stood out amongst the other girls of the island. Her long, black, wavy hair surrounded her like a mantle and her soft, dark golden skin glowed in the firelight. She loved the stories of her ancestors and had listened to the old woman tell them many times. But by far her favourite story was of the great sorceress, Ekewane. Rihani's large brown eyes held a faraway look as she listened to the story of her people.

Following the tribal war, there had been some disputes amongst the Islanders, but the chiefs of the tribes settled them without any further killing. A taboo against spilling human blood on the island had been put in place and no Islander would now kill another, for no one dared to break a taboo. If they did, they would be sacrificed on the stone altar on top of their sacred mountain to appease their gods so no great disaster would befall their island.

For a long time, Rihani sat looking at the dying embers. The storyteller and other members of the tribe had already returned to their huts. She watched her mother, Eigara, pick up a sacred ember and place it into a large shell. Only sorcerers were permitted to have the magic of fire, which was a gift from their gods in the sky. One day she also would take on that great role. Ekewane had also been 14 years old when she intervened and stopped the war. Rihani frequently reflected that she was now the same age as her ancestor. According to the customs of her people, she too would become a sorceress and help her people. She knew that it would only be through her that her people could remain safe from the dangers of the dark spirits that surrounded them.

"When you call on the spirit world, the words you say must be precise. The ointments and poultices must be made whilst using the correct spells. You cannot change them, for if you do, you could bring about great harm. They are the old words of our ancestors and you must remember them precisely," Eigara would constantly reiterate.

Rihani had also learnt to read the flight of the birds. Messages from their ancestors were often sent by birds.

Planting, deep sea fishing and other celebrations and sacrifices depended on the auspices of the birds. The ointments, poultices, medicines and chants used by the sorcerers on the island were jealously guarded, and only handed down through each generation of that family. Rihani knew that all the tribes had their own sorcerers, but the magic of Ekewane and her ancestors was more powerful than the others. She also knew that the other sorcerers envied her mother's power, for her family had proven again and again the great power of their magic.

Her mother, like the sorceresses before her, had sewn two small pouches for her daughters, similar to the one she herself wore around her neck. The bags were made of finely woven hibiscus leaves, bearing the intricate pattern of their tribe. Inside, she had put potent totems: shark teeth, the small bone of a tortoise that was their clan totem, the root of a sacred tomano tree, and a small bone that belonged to one of their forebears. These items helped Eigara and her daughters communicate with the spirit world and would also help ward off the dark spirits that surrounded them. Both Rihani and her sister Ema wore these pouches around their necks. Rihani would often subconsciously grasp hers and doing so always made her feel stronger and braver.

Although Rihani was told that she had magical powers in her blood, she was often tormented by doubts but was too afraid to voice her fears, even to her mother and sister. "What if the powers of my ancestors are not within me? Ekewane could see into the future, but I cannot. I may never be a sorceress like my mother and grandmother and my other ancestors. One day my people will depend on me and I may not be able to help them." As soon as she had whispered these words, a sense of foreboding sent cold shivers up Rihani's spine.

That night, when she finally fell into a fevered dream, she saw two blue eyes gazing at her. A white humanoid face surrounded these eyes, but the image was vague. Only the powerful eyes were distinct. She felt frightened and tried to run away, but the eyes would not release her. When she awoke the next morning, she felt even more perturbed. The eyes of her dream remained in her mind, glaring and intense. "It may be an ancestor from the spirit world," she thought. "Maybe it's a sign that I will join them soon." She shuddered, remembering again the potency of the eyes.

Chapter Three
Omen

The following morning, high-pitched shrieks vibrated down from the dark, ominous mountain at the centre of the island.

The people of the island had always heard these screams; they came from the spirits that lived on the sacred mountain and would at times come down to their villages. The eerie screams continued all the following day with terrifying intensity. In response to these screams, the sea that was regularly bright blue was dark and menacing.

Only the white froth of the high waves crashing against the jagged limestone reef gave any sign of colour.

The members of the tribe were heedful of the piercing cries. They cautiously went about their daily lives, never straying far from the village. Only Eigara, their great sorceress, could communicate with the spirit world and reassure them.

"There are both good and dark spirits living on the mountain. As long as we obey our taboos, venerate the spirits of our ancestors, and make sacrifices to our gods, we will not be harmed," she would often reassure them.

But even with these reassurances, the people on the island were still very much afraid of those terrible, haunting screams. Today, they were louder and more frightening, as if they were warning of darker days to come.

All day the strong wind that came from the sea tore through the tops of the high coconut trees that surrounded the island.
The strange sense of unease continued and the screams reminded them of how vulnerable they were.

They lived in a world of the supernatural and deep superstition and could only rely on their sorcerers to help them understand and survive.

The following night, the villagers sat around the large fire on the reef. The ear-piercing screams had subsided and the Islanders felt some relief. However, they only talked in whispers, still not at ease. The children, who at night usually played nearby, now sat quietly near their parents.

They too felt uneasy. Every now and again, the Islanders looked at the dark undergrowth surrounding their village. Darkness was the time during which they were more vulnerable.

Although it was hot and humid, they sat huddled

together, each a little more comforted by the contact of another person.

Then someone screamed, breaking through the murmuring sounds of the people sitting around the fire.

With trembling hands, the woman who screamed pointed to the night sky. The villagers looked up, horrified. At first they were too afraid to speak. Transfixed. Then screams erupted as more and more villagers became aware of the horrific sight.

High above, a trail of red flames could clearly be seen falling from the sky. Soon the whole tribe were on their feet screaming and wailing hysterically.

"WHAT IS HAPPENING? ARE THE GODS SENDING FIRE TO DESTROY US?" the people screamed as they pointed.

Eigara was also looking up. She too trembled at the imposing sight. She had never heard of fire in the sky before, and so sat there terrified.

"It could be the gods of the sky coming down to destroy us. Or it could be an omen, a sign of fire and blood. I must call to our gods and ancestors so that I may understand," she thought as she silently chanted the words of a powerful protective spell.

She suddenly felt cold. Deep within her, a terrible premonition overwhelmed her and she knew she would need all her strength and power to save her people.

Rihani was also looking up, mesmerised at the trail of fire falling from the sky. Strangely, she did not feel afraid like the other villagers around her.

"If it is the end of our people then I will not need

magical powers. I do not want to disappoint my family and people," she thought with a flicker of relief.

As these fleeting thoughts flashed through her mind, her heartbeat quickened. It pounded in an ever increasing rhythm, until she was afraid it would break through her chest.

She started trembling. The perspiration trickled down her face. Then, an excruciating pain spread throughout her body. She wrapped her arms around her stomach as she leaned over, unable to sit upright.

The pain was so intense that she could not breathe. She opened her mouth to try to ease her breathing but the air only entered her lungs in short gasps. Then her body, no longer able to sustain the pain, convulsed and she crumbled to the ground.

The world around her went black. Nobody sitting around the fire noticed Rihani. They were still screaming and looking petrified up at the sky.

Eigara, however, suddenly stopped her chanting for she felt her daughter's distress and quickly looked about for her. She finally spotted her curled up on the ground.

She then desperately tugged Aio, her husband, who was also staring bewildered at the sky, and pointed to Rihani.

"What happened to our daughter?" Aio asked anxiously, as they avoided the chaotic hysteria of the people and rushed to her side.

"I do not know. We must take her to her hut," answered Eigara, looking worriedly at Rihani's pale face.

Aio picked up his daughter and carried her to her hut, where he laid her carefully down on a mat and then left. He would wait for Eigara to explain about their daughter and what the fire in the sky meant.

He looked up again into the night and shivered. He did not understand what the fire meant, but he could feel that it was not a good sign.

Eigara finally came out of Rihani's hut. Her daughter had awakened and had eventually fallen into a fretful sleep.

"She has become a woman. The power within her is growing stronger. She must have felt the potency of the fire in the sky," Eigara explained to Aio, who was nervously pacing outside the hut.

He had many concerns about the future for his family and people.

"And what does the fire in the sky mean?"

"I do not know. I must invoke our gods so I may understand. But I feel it is not a good sign."

Eigara and Aio looked up again at the blaze high above them and slowly walked into their hut. It had been a difficult, disturbing night and it was a sign of things to come.

Sleep did not come to them or the other villagers on the island. They were too afraid that they would be burnt in their sleep. Only the children slept, unaware of the approaching danger

Rihani slept until late into the following morning. When she awoke, she found her mother sitting beside her. Her first thoughts were that she had been punished by their gods.

Evil thoughts had crossed her mind. She almost wished for the destruction of her people, because of her own insecurities and anxieties.

"What happened to me? A-and what does the fire in the sky mean?" she asked trying to hide her thoughts.

"I do not know what the fire means. I must continue to invoke our gods and ancestors to help me understand.

But, you are now a woman, You must stay in your hut and wear this special mat that has been blessed by our ancestors. The mat will protect you so that you may bear many healthy children.

Once you leave the hut ,you will wear this special, blessed belt like the other women on the island. Ema and your friends may come and keep you company, but you must not leave your hut. I will also come and teach you many things you now need to know and understand.

When the wet season arrives again, we will celebrate you becoming a woman. You will be a sorceress.

Now you must think of your future. Soon you will marry and we must decide who will be your husband."

Eigara smiled at her daughter and quietly left the hut. She hoped that they would be able to celebrate Rihani's initiation ceremony, but was still very much afraid for the future. She had to make more offerings to their gods and invoke their ancestors for help and protection.

Rihani lay on her mat feeling even more anxious.

"I am now a woman? What happened last night? I remember looking up at the fire in the sky and then my heart felt like it was being torn from my body. I felt an acute pain like I had never felt before. Those blue eyes suddenly flashed before me. They seemed angry because I had wished the destruction of my island, and then nothing," she sighed, feeling guilty.

The pain was still there, but the intensity had subsided.

"I am becoming a woman? My family and tribe will have even more expectations of me. And how can people think me a sorceress when I am so frightened and inadequate? I cannot marry!" she thought sadly.

Ema entered the hut, bringing flowers, fruit and a coconut shell filled with water. She was smiling. "Now we must pick a husband for you. You may pick anyone but Itu," said Ema shyly.

"Then we must think of the men that I can choose from," replied Rihani with a forced smile.

"My life will change. I do not want to be a sorceress. Everyone will expect me to be like my mother. I-I want something more. Something else. I cannot show anyone my fears. I have to pretend to be happy," she thought not listening to Ema who was chatting happily.

"There are many fine men on the island, especially Akua. All the men think you will pick them. I have heard them talking," giggled Ema, not realising Rihani was not listening.

They discussed the eligible men, but Rihani dismissed them all. She could not see any of them as her husband and she did not need another concern pressing her.

She wished she were more like Ema, who had already decided whom she would marry. Those blue eyes she kept dreaming about haunted her.

"Perhaps they belong to a spirit. The spirits may have already decided that I will never marry, but join them instead." Rihani felt her skin crawl as these thoughts flitted across her mind.

Every night, the burning streak across the sky reappeared. The people no longer sat around fires laughing and telling stories, but hastened to their huts so they did not have to look up at the phenomenon.

During the day they did not venture far from the village. Only groups of men went to the brackish pools to fetch drinking water.

Eventually, the day arrived when Rihani could leave her hut. After going down to a rock pool and bathing, she slowly walked towards her tribe who had gathered around her mother.

Although the fire in the sky was no longer visible, they were still too frightened to go about their daily lives as before. Many sat patiently for days near Eigara's hut, for only she had the power to explain and reassure them.

Finally, Eigara came out and faced the stone altar in front of her hut. She lifted her arms high above her head and started to chant. Rihani walked over and sat beside her sister Ema, and together they joined in the immemorial chant.

The ancient, rhythmic words resonated with power. "The power is in the words," Eigara would often repeat to her daughters.

The people of the village huddled around and watched Eigara perform her magic. She was calling to the spirits of their ancestors. A dark swirling mass billowed around the undergrowth as Eigara's voice rose above the wind whistling through the trees.

"Ai! Ai! Ai! I, Eigara, call to the spirit of Alubi, my great and powerful ancestor.

"Ai! Ai! Ai! I, Eigara, call to the spirit of Galudei, my great and powerful ancestor.

"Ai! Ai! Ai! I, Eigara, call to the spirit of Emenear, my great and powerful ancestor.

"Ai! Ai! Ai! I, Eigara, call to the spirit of Ekewane, my great and powerful ancestor.

"Ai! Ai! Ai! I, Eigara, call to the spirit of Kalibi, my great and powerful ancestor."

Eigara and her daughters repeated the chant over and over again, until she bowed her head in silence for a long time. Then, as if awakened from a hypnotic trance, slowly she turned to her people and said, "Our gods have warned us.

Once again, as in the time of our ancestors, our people will know great suffering and sorrow. Many of us will join our ancestors before our plight is over.

We cannot stop the pain that is to come. We can only plead to our ancestors for guidance and strength.

The spirits of the mountain have also warned us of the anger of the dark spirits that are to come."

The people remained spellbound. After a short pause, Eigara continued. "Until that day comes, we must continue to live as before, for we will need our strength.

Go and collect food, for our children must eat." Eigara then turned and staggered, exhausted, back into her hut.

Rihani and Ema knew that they too must join their mother and invoke their ancestors for help. Many strict taboos would be set in place once they entered the hut and started their sacred chants.

They could only drink a little water from the brackish pools, but food was forbidden and no one could enter the hut. Only at night could the girls return to their own hut and eat. Long, exhausting days lay ahead.

Rihani still felt apprehensive.

"What if our gods and ancestors punish our people because of me? My mother's power is strong. Although I will offer sacrifices, I do not think I will be heard." She felt dispirited that she was so inadequate and had to pretend to her mother and tribe.

Eigara gathered the dried roots of the sacred tomano tree and placed them in a large conch shell at the centre of her hut.

She then took her sacred embers and lit the roots. Smoke slowly swirled about the hut. All the while, she whispered a strange incantation.

The wisps of circling smoke created a strange, surreal atmosphere, purifying the hut and warding off evil spirits whilst they invoked their ancestors.

Eigara and her daughters sat cross-legged, rocking backwards and forwards to the rhythm of their chant. Their gazes transfixed on the smouldering embers as they went into a familiar trance, the chant transporting them into a strange dimension.

In the days that followed, the people of the village tried hard to ignore the continuous, penetrating screams that came down from the dark mountain.

The harrowing sound echoed throughout the

village. Ever increasing strong winds blew throughout the island, and dark ominous clouds hung low on the black, angry mountain.

Eigara had always reassured her people that the spirits on the mountain would not harm them. The women, however, were too afraid to leave the village to tend to their vegetable plots or fetch water from the brackish ponds which were further away from the village, up towards the side of the mountain. Only the men in small groups ventured beyond the village.

Head Chief Aio had also warned the tribe not to go fishing beyond the reef.

"The gods of the sea are angry. We must not go beyond the reef. I will send messages to warn the other villages around the island," he stated gravely.

When Eigara was not offering sacrifices to their ancestors and gods or chanting inside her hut, she would sit along the reef, watching the birds flying in the sky.

The villagers sat around their huts whispering and gazing at Eigara. They could hear the faint notes of a chant on the mournful wind.

Often, the interposing piercing cry from the mountain would drown out her chant. Eigara was calling her powerful ancestors and working her magic, and they felt some reassurance sitting close by her hut, even when they could not hear the mystical chant.

The people were very superstitious and nobody could ever recall hearing of a fire in the sky before. They could only rely on Eigara's magical powers to protect them.

Rihani and Ema were often also inside the hut,

praying with their mother.

"Together they are more powerful," the people whispered amongst themselves.

Chapter Four
Eigara and Aio

Eigara was known throughout the island as the Great Sorceress.

When other sorcerers could not heal a sick person, they went to Eigara for help. When dark spells had been cast, the victims would seek her out for counter spells, for all knew of her magical powers.

One day, her daughters Rihani and Ema would also inherit these powers. Because of these ancient powers, the Ramaoide class was proud to be the most potent class on the island.

Eigara had married very young, as was the custom of the island. She had three grown-up children and was still young enough to have more children.

The women married at fourteen or fifteen, and often the elder children would have children who were older than their youngest siblings. Eigara, like the rest of the people on the island, took pride and care in her appearance.

The men and women spent much of their time bathing and cleansing their bodies.

They bathed in the warm sea at least twice a day. They also massaged scented coconut oil over their bodies several times a day, and would comb coconut oil through their hair, in which both men and women wore flowers.

The Islanders took special pride in their bright white teeth, for these were considered a sign of beauty. They would brush them every day with a soft brush made from chewing the end of a small stick. Fine sand and seawater was then used as a paste.

All the Islanders had beautiful, clear, golden coloured skin and dark, shiny, wavy hair. The beauty of their bodies was extremely important to them.

The Islanders knew that if they did not conform to the required expectations, they would be shunned by the other Islanders.

When Eigara was young she had many friends. As she grew older and took on her role as a sorceress' apprentice, her friends, although outwardly friendly and cordial, distanced themselves from her. They had become fearful of her powers.

She was different from the other women on the island. She was a sorceress. People were intimidated by her power.

They would often avoid laughing and joking with her and only seek her out when they needed her help. It saddened her and sometimes she felt lonely, but like her mother and her ancestors before her, she had accepted her life.

Like her daughters, she too, when young, was much sought after by the young men on the island. She knew she was attractive, but many other girls were prettier.

Eigara, however, was also very wealthy and most importantly, she had powerful magic in her blood. Her parents had arranged her betrothal to Aio when she was still very young.

She had often watched him when he was not aware of her presence. Aio was handsome and very tall.

Even at young age, he stood out from other boys. When her parents had approached her with their decision that she should to marry Aio, she was overjoyed and was grateful to her parents for their choice.

Aio was taller and more powerfully built than the other men on the island. His long, dark hair reached below his shoulders.

Aio's presence in itself was one of power to be respected. Eigara loved her husband. His gentleness and wisdom never ceased to surprise her. When other chiefs were angry over disputes between the tribes, he would counsel them, always upholding justness.

He was widely respected. He was the Head Chief, as voted by all the chiefs on the island.

Rihani had inherited her tall stature from her father. She was taller than her sister Ema. Both sisters were considered beautiful.

They were members of the Ramaoide, the elite class, and one day they would inherit great riches in the form of land and coconut trees, as well as a powerful supernatural legacy.

Eiagara and Aio had planned to choose the future husbands for their daughters after their initiation ceremonies. However, many parents had already approached them, as the two girls were much desired by the other families on the island.

The boys of the Ramaoide class from throughout the island would be Eiagara and Aio's preferred marriage candidates, although the wealthy Enename of the middle class were also permitted to marry into the Ramaoide class.

However, the Sitio, or lower class, was frowned upon.

Aio and Eigara, like other Islanders, followed strict taboos, such as marrying someone from the same clan. Like all the people on the island, they obeyed these taboos in fear of retribution from their gods.

Eigara knew that Ema was the more tranquil of the two sisters and that her future would be more serene. She understood, however, that Rihani would ultimately want to choose her own husband.

She worried about her feisty, esoteric daughter, as she could see that Rihani often felt confused by the conflicting feelings within her.

She knew her daughter experienced overwhelming feelings of pride for her powerful heritage, fear that she would be unable to live up to the expectations of her family and people, and resentment at her life being strictly governed by traditions and customs.

Eigara understood these feeling for she too as a young woman had these internal struggles. Both her daughters would carry a heavy burden, for along with their power came great sacrifices.

Aio was very young when he knew he would marry Eigara. He belonged to the Enename class and was a member of the Iwa clan.

Their village was not situated near the sea like the other villages on the island, but around an inland lake.

Their tribe, however, had access to part of the shoreline so they were able to fish in the sea without asking permission from other tribes. Islanders were very possessive of the areas of shoreline allocated to them and other tribes needed permission to use these area to put their canoes out to sea.

Aio loved his village. The lake it surrounded was large and tranquil. The villagers used the water from the lake to drink, bathe in and fish for the much sort after milk fish.

The soil around the village was very fertile and the villagers did not have to travel far to fetch water and grow their taro, yams and other vegetables.

The village was also surrounded by high mango trees, which were the only ones on the island.

Aio, as a young boy, spent his time fishing and swimming like all the other boys of his age. Even at an early age, he stood out. Not only was he taller, but also friendly, caring and helpful to anyone in need.

He noticed Eigara when they were very young. He was a few years older than her. Villagers would often travel from one village to another to visit family and friends and he loved to visit Eigara's village.

He would often ask his parents if he could visit. The island was small, but sometimes it took the Islanders more than two weeks to complete their journey around it.

Events such as weddings, initiations and births were cause for great celebration and everyone on the island was invited. So it was that Aio would see Eigara often.

He knew she was different from other girls. She would often look sad and withdrawn. He knew she one day would be a sorceress and inherit great riches, but that did not matter to him.

When she celebrated her initiation ceremony, his

parents, like many others, approached her parents. The news that they had chosen him to marry Eigara did not come as a surprise.

He had always known that they were meant to be together. He would now make sure she would never be sad again.

Chapter Five
The Spirit World

Rihani looked at the frangipanis placed on the stone altar near the entrance of her mother's hut. Stone altars for their gods were built in each village, food and flowers were often left upon them in homage.

As was the custom on the island, the bones of their ancestors were buried around the huts of the village with large stones placed over the burial place. Some Islanders buried their dead within their huts. The remains of ancestors were highly revered. The bones had strong mystical powers and would help protect the family. When Ekewane died, she was lain down on a mat inside her hut. Her body was rubbed daily with scented coconut oil until only her bones remained. These bones still held strong supernatural powers which now belonged to Eigara and would one day go to Rihani.

The stone tombstones outside Eigara's hut were similar to others around the island and all families made special offerings to the spirits of their ancestors. It was at these tombstones that Eigara and her daughters now turned to for guidance and protection.

For many days, the three women sat inside the hut, singing their ancient chants handed down through the women of their family from the beginning of time. They invoked help from the spirit world: from their ancestors, from the spirits that lived in the mountain, and from their gods who lived in the sky and sea. The women were hot and thirsty for they could only drink small sips of water. They had not eaten since the night before and there was only a little breeze penetrating the woven coconut frond walls of the hut.

Finally, Aio ordered the men to prepare a large fire along the rugged shoreline as had been done on many nights before the terrifying fire in the sky. The people of the village understood that Eigara had spoken to the spirit world and she would explain what was happening. So as soon as the sun set, the people of the village gathered around anxiously waiting for Eigara. They looked up at the sky again and again to see if the fire had returned.

The sea was calm. The moon cast shiny rays across the rippling water. The mountain spirits had left and the village looked picturesque in the moonlight. Eigara, Rihani and Ema came out of the hut and slowly walked towards the anxious tribe. Eigara placed her sacred embers under the pile of dry leaves and watched as the fire started to burn, she then sat down beside her husband, Aio. As Head Chief, he was responsible for the safety of all the tribes on the island, but he relied on Eigara for guidance, for only she could communicate with their gods and the spirit world. The spirits had been angrier than usual and Aio had to know why. If the Islanders were in danger, they would depend on him. Many of the men, women and children from other tribes were also staying in the village. They knew that only Eigara could explain.

The Islanders were all looking anxiously at Eigara. This had not been the first time they had sat waiting for her to speak. They would often rely on her to tell them why the spirits of the mountain were so loud and angry, but this time there was also the fire falling from the sky. The people suspected that something was very wrong. Eigara had never before taken so long to explain what the spirits had communicated to her.

Rihani saw her brother, Gadiya, and his friend, Itu. She walked over to them and silently sat down, looking at her older brother. He was sixteen and already considered a man, as was his friend Itu, who was the same age. Next to him was her friend Adera, fifteen and betrothed to her brother. They would be married the following wet season. Her sister Ema was only a year younger than herself and sat next to Itu. Akua was also present. He was chief Dara's son from the Yarle clan, also a member of the elite Ramaoide class. Rihani knew that Akua hoped to one day marry her, so he would often visit her village, but the thought of marriage frightened her. It was another burden she did not want to think about.

Eigara sat silently as if still calling to her ancestors to give her courage. Her shoulders drooped and her head was bent. Her long hair shadowed her face and every now and again she would shudder. The tribe waited patiently. Rihani felt nervous. She could feel the tension surrounding her. Finally, Eigara lifted her head and looked into the fire. She spoke softly, but everyone could hear her.

"The spirits of our ancestors have spoken. Our gods are angry, for we will betray them. The spirits of the mountain have come to warn us. Our people have been in peace since the time of our ancestors, but now we are once again faced with great danger."

Rihani had never heard her mother sound like this. Her mother's voice was trembling and Rihani held her breath for what was to follow.

"What sort of danger?" asked one of the Islanders, gazing

intently at her.

"That, I do not know. The spirits did not tell me. But we must be very vigilant and strong. A dark, evil spirit is coming to our island," whispered Eigara.

"We are many and we are strong, and we will stop any danger coming to our island!" cried out the men.

"We cannot change our future. The dark spirits will come. No matter how strong our warriors are. We can only offer sacrifices to our gods and the great spirits to help us remain strong and survive what is to come." Eigara then bowed her head and started chanting.

The tribe members did not speak, but sat silently, listening to the chant for a long time, each contemplating their own fears for the future. Then quietly, one by one, they returned to their huts. They did not doubt the words spoken by Eigara and felt uneasy and afraid. Rihani stood up and sat next to her parents. Her brother and sister had left with the other members of the tribe. Akua waited for her, but when he realised she would not be leaving soon, he also retired disappointed. Rihani knew the repetitive chant her mother was singing was to ward off the evil spirits, and so she started chanting along with her.

"I will try to help my mother call upon our gods and ancestors. I must try to find the power within me that my mother said I have inherited," she thought obediently as she was chanting.

Both women entered into a trance-like state as they chanted the monosyllabic notes, swaying backwards and forwards in time with the sounds. They had become unaware of their surroundings and were lost in another world where time and place did not exist.

When the moon was high in the sky, they both stood up without muttering a word and returned exhausted to their huts. Rihani felt very tired, as the powerful chant had drained her of all her energy. But as she was walking towards her hut, she looked at the undergrowth surrounding their village. She had seen these trees and shrubs all her life, but tonight the dark shadows looked sinister and something seemed to be moving in the darkness. Rihani felt a cold shiver run up her spine and her heart beat faster and faster as she ran to her hut.

Breathlessly, she entered the hut she shared with her sister and some of her cousins. Rihani did not know who would be sleeping there tonight, for the children of the village often slept in different huts. Their parents were never concerned where the children slept, as all belonged to the village, most were somehow related, and they were considered one family. Tonight she felt safer sleeping in the crowded hut.

Rihani looked at Ema sleeping peacefully, and so lay down on her mat beside her. She still felt anxious. The high-pitched screams of the spirits of the mountain had returned, only now they sounded like a lament. She closed her eyes, listening to the even breathing of her sister. Eventually sleep consumed her.

Chapter Six
Premonition

"Rihani! Rihani! Rihani!"

Rihani woke up, startled. She quickly sat up and listened. Someone was calling her from outside the hut. It was a young girl's voice, but she didn't recognise it. She got up as if in a trance. The voice was pulling her outside. She looked around, confused. The sun was already high in the sky, but the village was deserted. She listened carefully for the voices of the villagers, but all she could hear was the strange, distressed crying of the young girl.

Rihani started walking along the beach, looking for the girl who was crying so agonisingly. She did not feel afraid. Further along the beach, she could see a strange grey mist. The voice was coming from within it. Upon reaching the thick blanket of mist, she hesitated momentarily before walking in. Rihani felt strange and nauseated. The thick mist tasted unfamiliar. She could no longer feel the warm sand or rough reef under her feet. There was no breeze from the sea, only a curious stillness, but she did not stop to question the strangeness of the situation. The wailing was pulling her further and further into the eerie, sickly mist.

Rihani kept walking until all of a sudden she stopped, incredulous. There were her people; their bodies scattered along the beach. Breathlessly she ran to the first body. It was a woman, but she was not recognisable. Her face and body were covered in sores and pus was oozing from them. Rihani looked around, terrified, All the bodies of the men, women and children were covered in these ugly boils. Some of the people were bloated and did not move. Their mouths filled with yellow and blood stained froth. Others were crying out in pain. She looked, horrified, at the images around her and then fell onto her knees and covered her face in despair. The smell around her was sickening. She had never smelled anything so foul. She wanted to vomit, but nothing would come out of her mouth. She could taste the acrid bile in her throat. Her body was trembling uncontrollably as the tears flowed down her face.

"Rihani! Wake up! "Rihani! Wake up!" came a voice from the distance.

Rihani looked around bewildered. Her sister was tenderly caressing and soothing her.

"You were crying out aloud in your sleep," whispered Ema.

Rihani looked around, perplexed, and then smiled hesitantly at her sister. It had only been a dream. "I-I am all right. It was only a b-bad dream. Go back to sleep."

"What was the dream about?" yawned Ema.

"I cannot remember," lied Rihani.

Ema hugged her and then lay back down on her mat. Soon Rihani could hear her soft, even breathing again. Rihani was too afraid to go back to her nightmare. She needed to speak to her mother. She knew instinctively that this dream was sent to her from the spirit world.

When the first rays of the sun started to gleam on the distant horizon, Rihani, exhausted, got up to search for her mother. She found her sitting near the reef, watching the horizon and deep in thought. She quietly sat down beside her.

"How can I describe what I saw?" Rihani thought. She was still afraid. Her throat was dry and sore as if she had been crying all night. She shuddered at the memory of those images.

Eigara was looking at the frigate birds flying around the dark clouds on the horizon. These clouds carried the spirits of the dead. "The dark clouds are amassing. They are preparing to carry many dead from our island," she thought despairingly.

Eigara became aware of Rihani and nodded. She waited silently for her daughter to tell her why she had awoken so early and had come looking for her. The shoreline was still deserted as the villagers were still asleep. Eigara had also had a restless night, afraid of what would come. Rihani had sought her out and she knew it must be important, so she waited patiently until her daughter could find the words to speak to her.

"I-I had a strange dream, but it did not seem like a dream, it felt very real," whispered Rihani. "I heard someone crying outside my hut. I went outside and started following where the crying was coming from. I walked along the shore and then saw a strange mist. I entered the mist and I heard people crying in pain. I saw many of our people lying on the sand. They were suffering, they were crying out in pain. I walked up to a woman. I did not recognise her because her body and face were covered in ugly boils. I looked at the other people lying on the beach. Th-they too were covered with these boils. It's like the sores were alive, coming from their mouths and eating their faces and bodies. I could see a dark, evil shadow eating their flesh.

The boils were flowing with thick yellowish pus. It did not stop, but just kept pouring out of their bodies." Rihani hid her face in her hands and started crying.

Eigara held her daughter in her arms and rocked her as she sang a soft chant to soothe her. After some time Rihani stopped crying and turned to her mother. "What was the meaning of this dream?"

"You are a woman. In you, the power of our magic is growing strong. Like Ekewane and some of our past ancestors, you have the gift of sight. You too can see things that will happen in the future. What the spirits have shown you will come about. There will be a time of great pain and sadness on our island. The fire in the sky and the spirits of the mountain are warning us against a great evil that will come. It will be the greatest evil we have ever faced and it may be the destruction of our people. The danger is not of men, but comes from the dark spirit world. We can only call upon our gods and the spirits of our ancestors that we may be strong enough to survive."

"I am afraid. I doubted the power of our ancestors was within me. I have always wanted to see into the future like Ekewane, but will I only see pain and destruction? I will suffer because of this gift, and I will be helpless to do anything. This magic is a curse!" cried Rihani.

"To be a sorceress, you carry an enormous burden. On our shoulders we carry a weight beyond time. The power of all our ancestors lies within us. Magic has always a price," whispered Eigara. She hugged her daughter and then bowed her head in silent plead to their ancestors.

Rihani sat there troubled. At first she had been afraid that she did not have the magic to be a sorceress, and now she was afraid because she knew that she did. Being a sorceress meant more than making poultices and healing the sick. Now that she had had a glimpse of her power, she was unsure whether she would be strong enough to bear this burden.

"Will I ever be happy and at peace like when I was a child?" she wondered sadly.

Eigara watched her daughter return to the village. What Rihani foresaw coincided with what she could see in the dark clouds on the horizon. "Many of us will soon die. I must return to the altar and offer more sacrifices to the gods to help us overcome this time of great sorrow," she whispered to the wind.

That morning Aio again sent messengers around the island to warn the other tribes of the imminent danger. The other members of his clan tried to go about their daily chores, but each was anxious about the future. The spirits of the mountain continued to howl all through that day and night, as well as the following day. The people of the island were becoming more and more apprehensive. As the days passed uneventfully, the Islanders began to relax. The spirits of the mountain had also quietened. The people cautiously returned to their daily lives, at first still very fearful. But as the days drifted, they became more courageous.

Rihani still felt shaken by her dream. She did not speak of it again, but she felt something had changed in her forever. Her carefree childhood days had ended. Long gone were the days spent laughing and playing with her sister and friends. Now she wanted to be alone. Ema had noticed the change in her sister, but knew that she could only wait until whatever was troubling Rihani had passed.

Chapter Seven
Arrival

Two large eels lay beside Rihani's brother, Gadiya, as he sat silently gazing into the horizon. Itu surfaced, holding up another speared eel. He threw the eel onto the reef and heaved himself up from the steep edge to join Gadiya. The two friends had been diving off the reef for moray eels. The eels lived in the underwater limestone crevices and were extremely dangerous to fishermen. They had a vicious bite. The only way to free yourself once bitten was to cut off their heads. The pain and damaged they inflicted left deep scars and at times caused death due to infection. The fishermen would skin the eels, cut them into pieces and eat them raw. Fish was only cooked for the very young children. Eels were a prized delicacy and were shared amongst the families of the village, who would sit together, laughing and enjoying the bounty. Food on the island was always shared amongst the tribe in this way.

"What are you looking at?" Itu asked, not seeing anything unusual in the distant horizon.

"That frigate bird keeps circling around the same spot, but I cannot see anything," replied Gadiya without taking his eyes off the dark shadow high up in the sky.

"It is probably looking at some fish."

"I do not think so. It has been circling the same place for a long time and has not dived into the water. I think I spotted a darker shadow in the water beneath it. I saw a glimpse of something darker when the waves rose higher.

"Then it is just a dolphin or whale. Are we going fishing out on the canoe?" asked Itu, beginning to lose interest.

Gadiya did not answer and remained sitting there quietly for a while. Then he got up and jogged back up to the huts on the shoreline, the eels forgotten on the reef beside Itu who looked baffled at his sudden departure. Normally, like Itu, Gadiya would not have taken any notice of such an event, but like the rest of the Islanders, he was now suspicious and wary of anything that did not look familiar.

Once Gadiya reached his parents he pointed to the horizon. "Mother! Father! Come and look!"

Aio and Eigara did not ask for explanations, but looked at their son and walked quickly with him to the reef. Some of the other villagers standing nearby also heard him, so they too followed curiously. Eigara looked at the distant frigate bird which was still circling above the waves. For a while she stood there, studying the bird without speaking. This bird was a messenger from the spirit world and sorcerers could interpret their messages.

"It is a message. The frigate bird is bringing us a message," she stated quietly without taking her eyes off the shadow high up in the sky.

Aio gazed at a distant silhouette that could now be seen bobbing up and down in the sea.It appeared and then disappeared as the waves ascended and descended.
"We will go out and see what it brings. We will take two canoes. And our spears," Aio commanded.
The Islanders who were standing around started murmuring amongst themselves were anxious to hear

what their chief was saying.

He turned and pointed to three of the men. "Get two canoes, your spears and some rope," he ordered.

Gadiya and Itu were disappointed that they had not been chosen, but nobody argued with the elders, and especially not with the Head Chief. So they waited on shore with the rest of the villagers who had gathered around, watching curiously. Among them was Akua who stood beside Rihani and watched the bird circling around the dark shadow floating on the horizon.

"It is probably only a dead shark or whale," Akua said, trying to reassure Rihani, for he noticed her trembling. Rihani, however, could not help feeling that something very significant was about to occur. Somehow, the dark shadow out at sea would involve her. She felt a strong premonition of inevitability.

Aio and his men steadily navigated their canoes beyond the dangerously ragged reef. Once beyond the reef, the waves kept pounding against the two small canoes, hindering their advancement. Finally, they managed to draw nearer and could see that the shadow on the water was in fact a small raft with something curled up on top of it. The nearer they paddled, the stranger the shape on the raft became. It looked human, but it was half wrapped in some tattered coarse material that was neither pig's skin, feathers nor grass matting. On some parts of the body, they could see raw flesh in a patchwork of different shades of red.

"What is it?" asked Kabit, a member of the clan.

"I do not know. It is very strange. It may be the spirit of an ancestor that has returned. We must take it back to

Eigara. She can tell us what it is," Aio replied cautiously.
"It smells terrible!" stated one of the men.
They silently looked at each other. They were afraid of
the spirit world and this strange creature looked and
smelled foul. "It is an evil spirit!" they whispered amongst
themselves.
"We must bring it back to Eigara!" ordered Aio. He too was
wary, but could not show his fear in front of his men.
They reluctantly paddled closer. Two of the men stood
on the outriggers of their canoes and cautiously reached
out to steady the raft. They shuddered at the vile smelling
creature. Aio, acting more confidently than he felt, tied a
rope around the raft and between the two canoes. He then
signalled that the raft was secured and ready to be towed
back to shore. The men did not dare touch the strange
creature, for it may have been taboo. Only Eigara would
know what it was.

High above, the frigate bird kept circling. The villagers
on the distant shore gazed spellbound at the scene. They
had seen the canoes reach the drifting shadow and could
see they were now accompanying it back to shore. When
they reached the reef, the men on shore helped pull the
canoes and the raft up onto the beach. The strange human
form was left on its raft until Eigara could tell them what it
was and what to do with it.
Eigara knelt beside the unconscious form. She chanted
softly as she raised her arms above the body. Her hands
hovered over it for a while as she continued chanting. The
villagers stood around her in a circle, awed by her mystical
powers. She finally slowly stood up and faced her people.
"This is not a bird or a spirit. It is a strange boy. He

has travelled far. An evil spirit possesses his body. Our ancestors want us to free him from this evil."

Rihani stood some distance away from the creature, too afraid to go nearer. Ordinarily she would be standing beside her mother, but something about this frightened her. Akua was still beside her and she felt grateful for his presence.

A small hut enclosed by a makeshift barricade was quickly erected, and although Eigara had stated that the creature was sent by the spirit world, Aio was guarded and would take no chances. The creature was carefully lifted out of the raft and taken to the hut. Some of women followed and helped lay him down onto a cool mat woven from green coconut leaves. Eiagara, in the meantime, called to her two daughters to follow her. Medicine and a poultice made of pig fat and various plants had to be carefully prepared. This would take them a while. The medicine had to be made with their sacred prayers, for it had to contain mana, the magic within all the ingredients, and their chant would call upon this magic. The potent medicine would contain the healing powers that were needed. Rihani wanted to object, but knew she could not, so hesitantly followed her mother and sister.

In the meantime two women from the village gently cleansed the body. They felt sickened by the smell, but now that they too could see that it was a boy felt sorry for the pain he was undoubtedly feeling.

When the poultice was ready Eiagara asked Rihani to come with her into the hut. Again, Rihani was overwhelmed by a strange feeling of inexorability. "I cannot go into the hut and help the creature inside," she thought looking around nervously. She noticed Akua frowning. He also did not want Rihani to enter the hut, but could not oppose for she was not yet his wife. After a few deep breaths, Rihani reluctantly entered the hut. She felt afraid. But when she saw the boy lying there unconscious, she felt silly. He was human and needed her help. She sighed, knelt beside him and lightly applied a poultice to his wounds, as Eigara showed her. Aio had stationed a man inside the hut, for he still felt uneasy. Akua was angry that he could not spend time with Rihani and he did not like the idea of her being in the hut with the strange boy. So he went to speak to Aio. "Aio, I do not think it is wise to let Rihani look after that strange boy. He may be possessed by an evil spirit," Akua stated.

"Rihani must learn to look after the sick. She is different from the other women on the island. She is a sorceress. However, she will not be alone in the hut. A warrior will always be present, so do not worry. Eigara has said that the strange boy is not a danger to us."

Akua knew he could not change Aio's mind. He still felt angry, but could do nothing. "One day she will be my wife and will do what I say!" he thought angrily as he stormed away.

Avery had a large wound on his leg, as well as other deep cuts on his back. The wounds had started to fester and pus was oozing through the flesh. Rihani felt sick. The smell was like in her dream, but she told herself that she must be brave. When they completed cleaning and dressing the wounds, the women sat beside the unconscious boy and started invoking their ancestors. Their chant contained the power that was handed down to them throughout time. It called the spirits of their ancestors to help drive the evil spirit away from the dying boy.

In the days that followed, Avery was given coconut water drop by drop so it could run down his throat. His body was constantly cleansed and fresh poultices were spread over the infected wounds. The rest of his body was gently massaged with sweet smelling coconut oil. The women massaged him from the top of his head down to his toes, for the evil spirit inside his body would leave through his feet. The coconut oil would also keep him warm. He was turned over on his stomach several times a day, so that all his body could be cared for. Avery remained unconscious, but Rihani had often seen him stiffen in pain.

"An evil spirit has been torturing this boy for a long time. Much cruelty has been done to him in his life," whispered Eigara as they looked at the multiple welts and scars on Avery's back.

Often, Ema, Rihani's younger sister, would also come into the hut and help care for Avery. She brought sweet smelling frangipanis and hibiscus flowers and placed them around the small hut so the smell would freshen the air. A guard was always nearby. At night, a group of men kept watch, sitting around a small fire outside the hut. Aio still felt uneasy about the mysterious intruder.

Finally, one morning Avery slowly came out of the darkness in which he had been entrapped for so long. There was no pain or fear in the darkness, and he did not want to leave it. He struggled to stay there, but a stronger force was pulling him back to the surface.

At first he could smell the air around him. All his life he had lived and worked amid filth, death and decay. The air in London had smelled septic and the orphanage where he stayed as a small child smelled of decay, mould and sewers. The tannery where he had worked smelled of the putrefying skins, while the whaling ship always smelled of death. The blood of the killed whales that spilled onto deck was often not washed off, whilst other parts of the whale's body were cut up and melted down for oil. Sometimes, parts of the whale were already rotting, by the time the last portions of blubber were finally melted down and stowed away in the barrels below. The air now around him was unfamiliar, sweet and salty. The smell enticed him to keep surfacing, but he was afraid. It felt like a strong invisible force was pulling him up from his deep abyss.

He slowly became aware of the sounds that surrounded him. There were gentle waves crashing against a reef, and a soft voice was singing, the notes soothing and caressing. "It's only a dream and I don't want to wake up," he thought, confused. But his mind kept picking up other sounds around him. There were harsh voices somewhere nearby. He could not understand what they were saying, but felt afraid.

He tentatively opened his eyes. At first, he only noticed the splashes of light that flickered through the walls of his hut. Then, as he began to distinguish his surroundings more clearly, he saw a strange woman sitting cross-legged beside him. He shuddered. There was something uncomfortable and powerful about the woman chanting beside him. He quickly looked beyond her and found himself gazing up into two large, soft, brown eyes. The girl was standing behind the strange woman. The chanting instantly stopped.

Rihani froze. She was in shock. Her stomach churned and knotted at the unexpected sight. Two blue eyes full of fear and pain were staring up at her. They were the same blue eyes as in her dreams. Avery looked, mesmerised, at the young girl. Then, unable to keep his eyes opened any longer, he slipped into a deep sleep.

"The evil spirit has left his body. He is asleep. The danger has passed. When he awakes, let him slowly drink the coconut milk," Eigara said to her daughter and then wearily stood up and left the hut, nodding to the guard outside the door.

Rihani watched Avery. Although he slept, she felt uneasy. The boy lying there was in great pain, for every now and again he would shudder and moan. Rihani's fear slowly faded as her heart went out to him. She understood that the pain was not only from his wounds, but went much deeper. She wondered who he was and how he came to be in the sea. She had always thought that her people were the only ones who existed and wondered if the spirit world had sent him, or if she herself had conjured him from her dreams.

Avery awoke, startled. He opened his eyes and saw he was still in the hut. The moon's rays were shining through the thatched walls and everything looked surreal. He looked around and could see the same strange woman still gazing at him. "I'm dreaming," he thought. His heavy eyelids closed again and drifted back to sleep.

The next time Avery opened his eyes, he saw the beautiful girl sitting and watching him. Disorientated, he gazed at the captivating image. He thought she had been in his dreams, but there she was. He tried to speak, but no sound came from his mouth. He wanted to sit up, but his body screamed out in pain, so he lay there and just gazed at the girl. She smiled shyly, gently lifted his head and put a shell containing a little coconut milk to his lips. As the thick sweet milk entered his mouth, he gulped at it. Rihani smiled and withdrew it, then offered it again. He understood that he must drink slowly, but he was so thirsty and had never tasted anything so wonderful in his life.

He had seen other native girls from a distance on the islands where the whaling ship stopped and traded for fresh water and food. But he had never seen anyone as beautiful as the girl sitting and smiling beside him. Her skin was golden and her long hair hung down below her waist in silky dark brown waves. He was entranced and did not want to lose sight of her. He struggled to keep awake, but his body felt so tired and he drifted off to sleep again.

As the days went by, Avery was slowly becoming familiar with the sounds and smells surrounding him. Every day, the women of the village would bring him food and water and help him eat and drink. He still felt uneasy when the strange woman visited him and checked on his wounds, for there was something different about her that frightened him. He was also wary of the kindness the Islanders were showing him. Nobody had ever treated him so kindly. He was suspicious that these natives might eat him, as he had heard stories of cannibalism from the sailors on the ship. However, he looked forward to the visits from the young girl he had first seen. He could not understand her speech, but was captivated by the sound of her soft, musical voice.

Rihani visited him often when he was unconscious. She still felt confused about the strange boy and tried not to think about him. However, once Avery was able to eat by himself, Aio stopped Rihani's visits. Akua was happy that Rihani no longer spent all her time in the strange boy's hut. He spent much of his own time in her company, trying to convince her that he would become her husband. Both of their parents had approved this union, so he felt confident. He accompanied her when she went to fetch the brackish water from the ponds and when she went fishing for octopus along the reef. They swam together and often sat along the reef talking and laughing.

Aio and Eigara smiled as they watch the couple spend time together. Soon Rihani would have her initiation ceremony and they could announce their betrothal. Rihani still did not want to think about her future. She knew why Akua was following her around, but felt confused about her feelings for him. At times she enjoyed his company and her future did not seem so difficult, but at other times, she wanted to be alone and hid from him. The boy in the tent was never far from her mind. When she remembered him unconscious and in pain, she felt as if he were expressing some of the demons that were also deep within her.

Avery slowly became stronger. Then the day had come when he was strong enough to leave the hut that had been his refuge for many months. With some trepidation, he looked forward to walking along the beach and making friends with other members of the tribe. He no longer thought that they would sacrifice him and he had missed the lovely girl sitting beside him. He knew he could no longer be isolated and reasoned that he would be able to meet her again once he was outside.

It was Gadiya and Itu who accompanied him out of his hut for the first time. As he slowly walked along the reef, he still felt dizzy. He had been in a dreamlike state for many weeks and nothing seemed truly real, although the sky and sea were a dazzling blue. The trees and shrubs were vivid green and he revelled in the simple natural beauty of his surroundings. He had always lived in dark and grey places. There was no colour in London. He could only remember the grey fog and smoke from the factories that left soot everywhere. Everything was dirty. The streets, houses and people all looked grey. The putrid smell of gutters full of sewage hung over everything, while the river, the factories and the people all smelled of rot. The city was festering in its decay. Here, all he could smell was the salt from the sea and the flowers in the trees that grew everywhere.

Had the ship been a bridge from one world to another? "I wonder if the cruel masters of my past lived here in this world, would they live peacefully like the Islanders or would they still be angry and cruel? Are things here on this island as wonderful as they seem?" Avery considered as he looked out into the sparkling blue sea. He did not notice the young girl hidden in the undergrowth, curiously watching him.

Chapter Eight
Trading Ships

Arrival of a Trading ship

As the days went by, Avery's health improved. Every morning he was helped down to the beach to a small pond near a high pinnacle.

The water in the pond seemed pink from the algae that grew on the strange limestone rock. Later on, he was told that the water there held magic healing powers, for this was where the first ancestors of the Eilu clan had appeared.

On this remote island in the middle of the Pacific Ocean, Avery experienced a peace unknown to him in the past.

The people were friendly, although it was difficult to understand their customs, rituals and strange beliefs in magic and spirits he could not see. He felt uncomfortable with the chanting, the stone altars and the stones in front of the huts that covered the remains of their ancestors.

Most of all, he was uncomfortable in the presence of the strange woman who was the village sorceress. He had often felt her eyes follow him, even though he could not see her.

Eigara was not old as he had imagined sorceresses to be. She was very attractive and had saved his life, but he still felt nervous around her.

He also hated seeing Rihani sitting in front of the stone altar, chanting. It distanced her even further from the world he had come from and understood.

Akua, unhappily, finally left to return to his village. He could no longer stay, for he had to return to his tribe.

However, he felt confident that after the wet season he would marry Rihani and move to her village. The women on the island owned the land and it was mainly the husbands who went to live in their wives' villages after marriage.

Rihani now had more free time and she often spent this with Avery. She felt confused, as on the one hand she wanted to avoid him, but on the other she was drawn to him.

Avery was different to her and she was curious to learn of the world outside of their island.

Avery always enjoyed spending time with Rihani. She had helped him learn to understand her language, which he did without difficulty.

When she finished her chores, she would sometimes seek him out and they would sit along the shoreline, talking.

At times Rihani's sister Ema would also sit with them and they would talk about their island home. The girls were also curious about the land Avery had come from.

Avery had only seen Aio's village and did not know how big the island was, nor how many people lived on it.

"Do you have oranges here?" asked Avery. He loved oranges and thought of the few pleasures he had tasted in the past.

"I do not think so. What are oranges?" replied Rihani.

"A toff on a horse once threw me an orange. It was the best thing I had ever eaten. I stole one once on board the ship. I got caught and beaten," Avery recalled.

"What is a 'toff' and what is a 'horse'?" asked Ema, confused at these strange sounds.

Avery laughed and thought for a moment before explaining. "A 'toff' is a rich man. And a 'horse' is like a chicken with four legs and a tail. It is as big as this." He jumped up in the air with his hands held high above his head to show the height.

"Do they eat you?" asked Rihani, perplexed. These creatures sounded very frightening.

"No, we eat them and make boots from them," laughed Avery again.

"'Boots'? What are 'boots'? asked Ema, even more confused.

"Things you wear on your feet," replied Avery.

"Why would you wear things on your feet?" asked Rihani, even more baffled by the curious customs of Avery's land.

"Don't know. You just do." Avery felt exasperated trying to explain.

Rihani looked up at the night sky and wondered about the strange place had Avery come from. What horrible place it must be, with chickens as big as houses and all those scars on his body.

"Avery, father wants me to help mother smoke you," Rihani announced after a short silence.

"Smoke me? What do you mean smoke me? In a pipe?" Avery laughed in a high-pitched hiccup.

Rihani looked at him calmly and continued. "It is very serious. We will call upon our gods so they may decide if you can become one of us."

"Is this about me?" Avery was now concerned.

"Yes. We will collect dried coconut leaves, for they are a gift from our gods. We also need the black ink from the octopus," explained Ema.

"Father will tell you this. He will also tell you to catch a black noddy bird. You must keep it with you and feed it for the next ten days.

Then you must kill it. The blood is poured over our sacred pinnacle and Mother will be able to read the blood.

After that, we smoke you for three days and three

nights. If our gods accept you, you will become one of us," continued Rihani.

"W-what if your gods don't like me? A-and when will this happen?" Avery asked fearfully.

"If our gods do not accept you, you will be put on a canoe and sent back out to sea. Mother will tell us when the moon is right for the ritual," explained Ema.

Rihani looked sadly at Avery. He had the same blue eyes as in her dreams, but listening to him, she understood that there were many men like him where he came from.

Maybe he was not the one in her dreams? Their gods would determine if he could stay. She liked Avery, but she also believed in the wisdom of her gods and the spirits of her ancestors.

Rihani and Ema left Avery deep in thought. He had finally thought he was safe, but felt foolish in believing that his future would be better than his past. He liked Rihani and thought of her as a friend.

She smiled and laughed with him, but there was something mysterious about her too. He could sense a darkness deep within her.

He had sensed this darkness in Eigara, her mother, and for the first time since arriving on the island, he felt apprehensive.

As Avery gained his strength he walked further around the shoreline by himself, it was the first time in his life that he felt freedom. Nobody was watching him to make sure he kept working.

However, Rihani's words kept returning to his mind.

"I may not be able to enjoy this freedom for much longer. What will happen to me if I'm put back out to sea?" He was afraid.

Aio had not approached him with any mention of 'being smoked', so although he felt uneasy, Avery wanted to enjoy as much as possible his time on the island. It was the first time he could enjoy the warm sun on his body.

It was also the first time in his life he had time to reflect. He thought about Rihani.

"She's very different from the women I've seen in London. Like all the people I've seen on this island, she seems to be naively happy. They are unaware of the world beyond their island. But she also has this strangeness about her. It's as if she 'knows' something others don't."

In the meantime life, on the island was peaceful.

The people were friendly, and Avery often wondered if he had really died. The island was paradise and he wanted to remain here.

He did not want to be 'smoked'. One day, as he was sitting outside the hut that he now shared with Gadiya, Itu and other boys of the village, he heard a terrifying, wailing scream. It seemed to come from the intimidating mountain that shadowed the island.

The scream echoed throughout the huts of the village. He froze, too afraid to even breath. The wailing turned into a high-pitched scream and he felt the hair on his body stand.

He anxiously looked around at the other people in the village. They too had stopped and were silently gazing towards the mountain.

The screaming continued for a while, and then

slowly started to withdraw back up the mountain. To Avery's surprise the people then continued what they were doing as if nothing had happened.

He felt shaken. Seeing Gadiya and Itu coming back from fishing, he walked quickly towards them.

"Gadiya! Itu!" he called out.

Gadiya and his friend nodded to Avery as they approached him.

"W-what… w-what was t-that s-scream?" stuttered Avery.

"Mountain spirits. Do not be afraid, they will not harm you," replied Gadiya as he continued walking.

Avery was still shaken. As he walked along the sea, he could not help but think,

"If there are spirits that live in the mountain, what do they eat? The only meats on the island are the birds, pigs and chickens. Do the spirits lure people onto the mountain and then eat them?"

Could it be that he was mistaken about the natives? Would they sacrifice him to the spirits on the mountain? He shuddered and felt the familiar fear he had lived with for many years returning to him again.

That night as he sat beside Rihani and Ema, he hesitantly asked them about the spirits he had heard that day.

"Have you ever seen the spirits that live on the mountain?" he asked.

"Sometimes we see a haze twisting around our village. We know that it is a spirit coming down from the mountain and we stay inside our huts. Although my mother says that they will not harm us, we must obey and stay inside," replied Rihani a little nervously.

Avery noticed that both Rihani and Ema shuddered. "They too are affected by the intense screams," he thought.

"Women are not allowed to go up onto the mountain, only the men can go. They hunt noddy birds and cut down the great tomano trees to make dugout canoes," explained Rihani.

"But we can go part way up to collect the pandanus fruit," continued Ema.

"W-what do spirits eat?" Avery asked suspiciously.

"Spirits? They do not eat anything," replied Rihani.

"So th-the spirits come down from the mountain to check on you and make sure you obey? Obey what?" asked Avery.

"Well, yes. We must obey our taboos and pray to our gods and ancestors. But the spirits also come down to the sea for cleansing," replied Rihani.

"Cleansing?" asked Avery, doubting what he was hearing.

"It is a cleansing wind that carries the spirits off the mountain and out to sea. The wind has power and can do that. The spirits will return to the mountain of course, because that is where they live," replied Rihani.

"What about rain? Doesn't rain cleanse the mountain?" asked Avery, even more mystified.

"The gods in the sky give us rain and feed the land so things will grow. But only the sea can heal and cleanse.

When we are sick, we bathe in the sacred pool in the sea. When you wash a baby in the sea, the baby will cry.

That is what happens to the mountain. The mountain is crying because it is being washed and cleansed by the spirits that live there."

"How do you know all this stuff?" said Avery. "The spirits cleansing the mountain?" He was sceptical and believing at the same time. Some things on this island were unexplainable.

"When the mountain cries, we know it is crying because it is being cleansed. But when the screams are angry, we know the spirits are angry with us or are warning us.

Only our mother and the other sorcerers and sorceresses can speak to the spirits. One day, Ema and I will also speak to the spirits," replied Rihani proudly.

Avery was more than a bit confused and fearful too. He had never thought much about spirits or ghosts before.

He had been in a church in London once, but he did not like it and got out. He heard tales about banshees and the Little People from some of the sailors, but such things were not for him.

For Avery, religion and beliefs were for 'toffs'. Yet on this island, things were different. Things like the spirits, the ominous mountain, the smoke and the ability to 'read' the birds. "Hell!" he said.

"I just don't know." Rihani was different too, he knew. Different and somehow special.

Finally, the day had come. Aio approached him early one morning. "Avery it is time."

"T-time?" asked Avery, although he suspected that

his 'smoking' would be delayed no longer.

"You are now no longer weak. We must see if our gods accept you as one of us. Today, I will show you how to catch a noddy bird. You must care for this bird. If it dies, a black spirit resides in you and you must leave the island. We will also cover you with the black ink of the octopus and this will protect you. After ten days, you will kill the bird and Eigara will spill the blood over our sacred pinnacle. You will stay in your hut for three days and three nights and we will use the smoke of our sacred tree to ward away any evil spirit that still lingers in you. Once the three days are over, Eigara shall read the blood on the sacred pinnacle of our ancestors. If the gods have accepted you. You will remain here as one of us."

Avery felt frightened. He looked at Rihani who was standing near her hut. She smiled at him. Somehow this gave him courage. He could feel her gaze as he unwillingly followed her father to learn how to catch a noddy bird with a net attached to a long pole. This was something he had never done before and he was sure he would make a fool of himself. He did indeed have difficulties catching the bird, but with Aio's help, he finally managed it. The first step of his ritual was completed. Aio then put the bird in a small cage for Avery to carry.

He was taken to a special hut. Eigara and Rihani entered soon after. They painted his body with the black ink of the octopus. As they dipped their fingers in the ink, they chanted a strange invocation. The chant sent shivers up his spine. When they left he looked at the strange patterns they had designed all over his body. He knew he could leave his hut, but felt exhausted and so lay back down on his mat and slept. He dreamt of Rihani. She was in the form of a strange, silvery haze. He tried to follow her, but when he was in reach, she slipped further away. The next morning, he left his hut in search of Rihani. He found her but she looked away as if he were a stranger. He did not understand why. "She's avoiding me. She was my friend," he thought sadly. He felt alone and spent his days roaming the shoreline carrying the caged noddy bird.

On the tenth day, Avery was summoned. He was told to stand over the stone altar and kill the noddy bird. The blood was collected in a coconut shell. Avery's stomach lurched at the thought of killing his pet bird, as he had become rather attached to it. He wanted to refuse and free it, let it fly away, but he knew that it would be his life or the bird's.

Eigara, Rihani and Ema stood beside him and chanted. At first the chant was slow, but it slowly became louder and faster until he could feel the pounding of his heart. He took the small bird, closed his eyes and cut off its head, letting the blood drip into the bowl. He had never killed anything before. He felt sick and had to fight to keep the bile in his stomach. Perspiration was running down his body, leaving strange streaks as it ran into the black ink.

Avery thought he would break, he was so tense. Then he felt a soft hand touch his arm and he opened his eyes. Rihani stood there and motioned for him to follow her. He followed her into his hut and there in the centre a fire was burning. The hut was only lightly smoky and was surprisingly not unpleasant. He collapsed onto his mat and placed his hands into his face. He did not want to see anyone. He wanted to be alone. Eigara, still chanting, took the blood down to the sea. There she poured it over the sacred pinnacles and then left.

For three days Avery stayed in his hut. Food and water as well as dry leaves were left outside his hut. It was up to him to keep the fire going. His sleep was restless as he had to constantly put leaves on the fire to keep it smoking. He felt hot and dirty. He had not bathed since the day the ink was painted on his body. The streaks on his body reminded him of when he worked in the tanning factory. Somehow, he began to think about his time in London. "Maybe it wasn't that bad after all," he thought despondently.

Finally, one morning Gadiya came into his hut and told him to follow him to bathe in the sea. He noticed the people of the village standing around the stone altar. Eigara, Rihani and Ema were sitting cross-legged in front of the altar chanting. When he finished bathing, he was taken to the stone altar. He felt his heart beat in trepidation of what was to follow. His life now depended on what Eigara would say. He looked down at Rihani. She had her eyes closed and he felt a strange stirring within him. "I can't leave her," he thought as he too closed his eyes to the sound of the repeated monotone words of the chant. He started to relax, lulled by the chant that seemed endless. Avery was startled as Eigara voice broke into his consciousness. She was now standing in front of him.

"The gods have spoken. The evil spirit that lived within you has left. Our ancestors have accepted you. You may live on our island. You must obey our taboos, or you will be punished." She then turned and walked into her hut.

"It's over," thought Avery with overwhelming relief. He looked at Rihani and she beamed at him. She stood up and walked towards the sea. Avery quickly followed and together they strolled along the reef without speaking.

As the months passed, Avery could communicate fluently with the tribe. The people were curious and asked him many questions about where he came from. They would sit around the fire at night and listen to him talk about the far away land he had come from.

"Many people live in large villages called 'towns'. Larger villagers, like the one I came from, we call 'cities'. The 'cities' are so big and the buildings so high that the sun is hidden, and people live in the shadows. The air is not sweet like on this island, but always smells like sewage and filth. The sky is very rarely blue. It's mostly grey. At night you cannot see the stars, because everything is covered with a thick smoke. Some people have too much food and other things, whilst others die because they have nothing, not even enough to eat. So people fight and kill so they can survive. Here on your island, it's always warm. But where I came from it can be very, very cold, and people die because of this cold. Here, people do not kill each other for food or greed. You are very fortunate," Avery would often recount sadly. However, at times, almost unbelievably, he missed that old, familiar world.

Although the Islanders could not visualise many of the things Avery was describing, they were fascinated by his stories. For a long time, they had believed that they were the centre of the world. They were aware of the existence of some other islands, for over time a few canoes that were lost at sea had beached on their Island.

But the stories told by Avery of distant lands populated by so many people were just incredible.

Avery often went fishing beyond the reef with Gadiya and Itu in their canoe. It was on one of these trips that they saw a ship on the horizon. Gadiya and Itu became afraid, for they thought it was a monstrous sea bird.

"It's not a bird. It's a large canoe called a 'ship'. But the men on the large canoe can be very dangerous," Avery informed the other two boys. He felt a strange sensation in his stomach as his past fears flooded back to him. He felt an acute depression and a sense of foreboding taking hold. "If they find me, they will take me back. They may even hang me for desertion," he thought.

The boys quickly paddled back to shore to find Aio and the elders of the tribe. They knew that they were in imminent danger, for they had been waiting for an evil spirit since before Avery's arrival. This monstrous canoe with its strange wings could be the vessel bringing the evil spirit with it. Eigara stood beside her husband and other members of the village as they watched on the distant horizon the large dark silhouette approaching their home. She slowly turned to her people and stated gravely, "The time has come." Then she turned around and went inside her hut where she sat and called to their ancestors for help.

Avery looked around and said, "It's a large canoe called a 'ship'. On board there are many men and they can be very dangerous. On some islands, men go ashore and trade for water, meat, fruit and fish, and they leave without causing harm. But on some ships, the men go on shore and kill the people living there." Avery shuddered. Perhaps this ship had come to take him back? He looked around to see where Rihani was, then went and stood beside her. She then surprised him by slipping her trembling hand into his. For the first time in his life he felt strong and protective of Rihani who always seem so spirited and proud.

That night chief Aio called a meeting.

"While these strange men are on our island, the women and children must hide in the caves. I will send messengers to the other tribes on the Island to warn them to do the same."

"We should leave now!" cried the women.

"No, the reef is dangerous and will guard our village during the night. Tomorrow you will leave when the sun rises. Tonight, prepare food and water to take into the caves," Aio ordered.

That night the people of the village were too afraid to sleep. "These strangers may have powers that would allow them to pass through the reef and kill us in our sleep. Avery has told us stories of the wondrous powers of these men," they whispered to each other. Aio also felt distrustful. He stationed two men to stand watch. The moon was high and they could see if anyone approached the reef.

Rihani lay beside Ema in their hut. She had no doubts that the world they had known until now would change. "Dark spirits are arriving on our island." She trembled at the thought and her tears flowed. She saw again the imagines of her people dying on the shore. She had felt safe with Avery's hand holding hers, but now she was alone and her dream came back to her. She wanted to run from her hut and find him so she would not feel so afraid, but knew that she could not.

Early the next morning, the women and children packed their belongings and headed quickly up to the caves on the side of the dark mountain. There they met the women and children from some of the other villages. They hid in the limestone caves and anxiously waited until Aio would send a messenger to tell them they could return to their villages.

Eigara, Rihani and Ema, together with other sorceresses from the nearby villages, sat in a circle and called to their gods and ancestors to protect them. Eigara invoked her ancestors as she swayed backwards and forwards in time with her chant. Her ancestors were the most powerful on the island and only with their help would she know if their men would be safe. The sounds of the voices around her disappeared as she entered further and further into her trance. She could see the men gathered on the beach, but felt that they were in no imminent danger. Relieved she slowly withdrew from her trance-like state.

The captain of the Victoria sailed the whaling ship slowly towards the island. The sea was uncharted in this part of the world and the island itself was not shown on his map of the Pacific. From what Captain Fitzsimons Caines could see from his telescope, the island was small with a high towering mountain in the centre. It was lush with vegetation and he had seen fires along the coastline the night before, so he knew it was inhabited. Captain Caines was not too pleased to have to stop at another inhabited, uncharted island, but he needed fresh water and food. He hoped that the natives were friendly.

He could see that a dangerous reef surrounded the island, so gave orders to anchor the ship and lower two boats. They would have to row a long way in to shore. He knew that if they had to leave the island quickly, they would be exposed for a longer period of time due to their distance from the ship. Twelve members of the crew boarded the boats and rowed cautiously to the shoreline. The men were heavily armed. They knew that on some islands, the natives were hostile and there was always the risk that they could become food themselves.

Head Chief Aio and the other men of his tribe waited patiently on the beach. Other chiefs and members of the nearby villages also joined Aio. The chiefs all wore their finest adornments to show their power, and to ward off evil spirits in time of battle. Whale teeth were proudly worn by the chiefs. These were the most sought after of adornments, for they represented strong powers and only the chief of each tribe was permitted to wear them.

The natives felt confident that they could defeat any aggression by the strange men coming towards them in the large canoes. However, Avery had warned them that these men would carry guns. His explanation of a gun was not truly believed, but the men were very suspicious nevertheless. Avery had also explained about metal knives and bayonets, so although the men were confident that they far outnumbered the men coming ashore, they still felt apprehensive.

Once on shore, Captain Caines stood flanked by all but two of his men, who were ordered to wait near the boats. When he spotted Avery, he felt somewhat relieved.

"If a white boy lives here with these natives they should not be dangerous, and maybe we can communicate better with them," he thought as he walked cautiously towards them.

Avery stood behind Aio and the other chiefs. He was still afraid these men would take him back. He had not completed his contract so was wary of the men. As soon as the captain and his men approached the tribe, Aio turned to Avery and nodded. Avery knew that he could not hide, but had to communicate between the two parties.

"Welcome to our island," he said, translating Aio's words to the captain.

"We come in peace," replied the captain.

"Why have you come?" asked Aio, and Avery translated.

"We need fresh water and food for our ship. We can exchange great gifts for your food." The captain looked around suspiciously. There were about two hundred men on the beach, but no women or children.

"We will give you food. What gifts have you brought us?" asked Aio. The captain then ordered two of the men to fetch the hatchets, knives, mirrors, beads, tobacco and two guns from the boats. He demonstrated to Aio and the natives the power of the rifles. This was also a way of showing them their superior power. He lifted the loaded gun and pointed it to an overflying bird and then pulled the trigger. The noise itself frightened the natives, and when they picked up the dead bird they were awestruck at the magic of this new weapon.

The Islanders looked in amazement at the other goods to be exchanged, for they had never seen such wondrous things before. Aio and the other chiefs were pleased, so they began to barter for the goods. A pig was worth a hatchet, and then there were chickens, coconuts, taro and pandanus fruit. Most exciting of all to the Islanders were the guns, which were exchanged for dried coconut flesh called copra. The Islanders had learnt to dry coconut flesh and stored it to use in times of drought which happened every few years. Once the bartering was completed, the first load of food was brought forward and loaded onto the boats.

The exchange had taken all day. When the sun was beginning to set, the captain and crew returned to their ship with the plan to revisit the island on the following day. The Islanders were friendly, but experience had taught Captain Caines sailors who stayed onshore could be killed during the night, leaving the natives to keep both the goods and food.

In all, the exchange took two days to complete. Water was carried from the brackish ponds and emptied into the ship's barrels. Cages for the pigs and chickens were built and the fruit and vegetables were stored in large crates. Finally, the captain was well pleased with his reception and the exchange of goods and pulled the Victoria back out to sea. He made a note in the Captain's logbook: "The island looks small. A mountain lays at the centre of the island, probably an old volcanic crater. Because of the low lying clouds, we could not determine how high the mountain actually was. A dangerous reef surrounds the island. About two hundred men participated in the exchange. No women or children were in sight. An English boy was seen living with the natives. His name and circumstances remain unknown. The boy, however, helped facilitate the trade as he could speak the native tongue. The natives were very friendly but naive. They were astounded by our superior goods and were more than willing to exchange these for food and water. I have named the island Volcano Island."

Aio and the rest of the Islanders watched the ship disappear into the horizon. Then he turned to the men. "We have many new things that will help us. The hatchets and steel knives cut better than our clam axes. The guns are very powerful. If more of these strange men return and attack us, we will defend ourselves better. I am happy with the exchange, but I am glad these men have left our island. It is time to call our women and children home, and for all tribes to return to their own villages."

Rihani, Ema and the rest of the women anxiously returned to their villages. They were curious about the arrival of the men on the big canoe with the large white wings. That night there was a great celebration. A large pig was killed and cooked in an underground oven. Taro, sago and other vegetables were wrapped in coconut leaves and placed over the pig to be cooked as well. Everyone was happy. There was singing and dancing all night. The men happily chewed the bitter tasting tobacco that was given to them by the men from the large canoe. Avery, however, did not join in the celebration but sat alone on the reef. He felt a deep sense of foreboding.

Chapter Nine
The Cannon

As the days went by, Avery's health improved. Every morning he was helped down to the beach to a small pond near a high pinnacle. The water in the pond seemed pink from the algae that grew on the strange limestone rock. Later on, he was told that the water there held magic healing powers, for this was where the first ancestors of the Eilu clan had appeared.

On this remote island in the middle of the Pacific Ocean, Avery experienced a peace unknown to him in the past. The people were friendly, although it was difficult to understand their customs, rituals and strange beliefs in magic and spirits he could not see. He felt uncomfortable with the chanting, the stone altars and the stones in front of the huts that covered the remains of their ancestors. Most of all, he was uncomfortable in the presence of the strange woman who was the village sorceress. He had often felt her eyes follow him, even though he could not see her. Eigara was not old as he had imagined sorceresses to be. She was very attractive and had saved his life, but he still felt nervous around her. He also hated seeing Rihani sitting in front of the stone altar, chanting. It distanced her even further from the world he had come from and understood.

Akua, unhappily, finally left to return to his village. He could no longer stay, for he had to return to his tribe. However, he felt confident that after the wet season he would marry Rihani and move to her village. The women on the island owned the land and it was mainly the husbands who went to live in their wives' villages after marriage. Rihani now had more free time and she often spent this with Avery. She felt confused, as on the one hand she wanted to avoid him, but on the other she was drawn to him. Avery was different to her and she was curious to learn of the world outside of their island.

Avery always enjoyed spending time with Rihani. She had helped him learn to understand her language, which he did without difficulty. When she finished her chores, she would sometimes seek him out and they would sit along the shoreline, talking. At times Rihani's sister Ema would also sit with them and they would talk about their island home. The girls were also curious about the land Avery had come from. Avery had only seen Aio's village and did not know how big the island was, nor how many people lived on it.

"Do you have oranges here?" asked Avery. He loved oranges and thought of the few pleasures he had tasted in the past.

"I do not think so. What are oranges?" replied Rihani.

"A toff on a horse once threw me an orange. It was the best thing I had ever eaten. I stole one once on board the ship. I got caught and beaten," Avery recalled.

"What is a 'toff' and what is a 'horse'?" asked Ema, confused at these strange sounds.

Avery laughed and thought for a moment before explaining. "A 'toff' is a rich man. And a 'horse' is like a chicken with four legs and a tail. It is as big as this." He jumped up in the air with his hands held high above his head to show the height.

"Do they eat you?" asked Rihani, perplexed. These creatures sounded very frightening.

"No, we eat them and make boots from them," laughed Avery again.

"'Boots'? What are 'boots'? asked Ema, even more confused.

"Things you wear on your feet," replied Avery.

"Why would you wear things on your feet?" asked Rihani, even more baffled by the curious customs of Avery's land.

"Don't know. You just do." Avery felt exasperated trying to explain.

Rihani looked up at the night sky and wondered about the strange place Avery had come from. What horrible place it must be, with chickens as big as houses and all those scars on his body.

"Avery, father wants me to help mother smoke you," Rihani announced after a short silence.

"Smoke me? What do you mean smoke me? In a pipe?" Avery laughed in a high-pitched hiccup.

Rihani looked at him calmly and continued. "It is very serious. We will call upon our gods so they may decide if you can become one of us."

"Is this about me?" Avery was now concerned.

"Yes. We will collect dried coconut leaves, for they are a gift from our gods. We also need the black ink from the octopus," explained Ema.

"Father will tell you this. He will also tell you to catch a black noddy bird. You must keep it with you and feed it for the next ten days. Then you must kill it. The blood is poured over our sacred pinnacle and Mother will be able to read the blood. After that, we smoke you for three days and three nights. If our gods accept you, you will become one of us," continued Rihani.

"W-what if your gods don't like me? A-and when will this happen?" Avery asked fearfully.

"If our gods do not accept you, you will be put on a canoe and sent back out to sea. Mother will tell us when the moon is right for the ritual," explained Ema.

Rihani looked sadly at Avery. He had the same blue eyes as in her dreams, but listening to him, she understood that there were many men like him where he came from. Maybe he was not the one in her dreams? Their gods would determine if he could stay. She liked Avery, but she also believed in the wisdom of her gods and the spirits of her ancestors. Rihani and Ema left Avery deep in thought. He had finally thought he was safe, but felt foolish in believing that his future would be better than his past. He liked Rihani and thought of her as a friend. She smiled and laughed with him, but there was something mysterious about her too. He could sense a darkness deep within her. He had sensed this darkness in Eigara, her mother, and for the first time since arriving on the island, he felt apprehensive.

As Avery gained his strength he walked further around the shoreline by himself, it was the first time in his life that he felt freedom. Nobody was watching him to make sure he kept working. However, Rihani's words kept returning to his mind. "I may not be able to enjoy this freedom for much longer. What will happen to me if I'm put back out to sea?" He was afraid.

Aio had not approached him with any mention of

'being smoked', so although he felt uneasy, Avery wanted to enjoy as much as possible his time on the island. It was the first time he could enjoy the warm sun on his body. It was also the first time in his life he had time to reflect. He thought about Rihani. "She's very different from the women I've seen in London. Like all the people I've seen on this island, she seems to be naively happy. They are unaware of the world beyond their island. But she also has this strangeness about her. It's as if she 'knows' something others don't."

In the meantime life, on the island was peaceful. The people were friendly, and Avery often wondered if he had really died. The island was paradise and he wanted to remain here. He did not want to be 'smoked'. One day, as he was sitting outside the hut that he now shared with Gadiya, Itu and other boys of the village, he heard a terrifying, wailing scream. It seemed to come from the intimidating mountain that shadowed the island. The scream echoed throughout the huts of the village. He froze, too afraid to even breath. The wailing turned into a high-pitched scream and he felt the hair on his body stand. He anxiously looked around at the other people in the village. They too had stopped and were silently gazing towards the mountain. The screaming continued for a while, and then slowly started to withdraw back up the mountain. To Avery's surprise the people then continued what they were doing as if nothing had happened. He felt shaken. Seeing Gadiya and Itu coming back from fishing, he walked quickly towards them.

"Gadiya! Itu!" he called out.

Gadiya and his friend nodded to Avery as they

approached him.

"W-what . . . w-what was t-that s-scream?" stuttered Avery.

"Mountain spirits. Do not be afraid, they will not harm you," replied Gadiya as he continued walking.

Avery was still shaken. As he walked along the sea, he could not help but think, "If there are spirits that live in the mountain, what do they eat? The only meats on the island are the birds, pigs and chickens. Do the spirits lure people onto the mountain and then eat them?" Could it be that he was mistaken about the natives? Would they sacrifice him to the spirits on the mountain? He shuddered and felt the familiar fear he had lived with for many years returning to him again. That night as he sat beside Rihani and Ema, he hesitantly asked them about the spirits he had heard that day.

"Have you ever seen the spirits that live on the mountain?" he asked.

"Sometimes we see a haze twisting around our village. We know that it is a spirit coming down from the mountain and we stay inside our huts. Although my mother says that they will not harm us, we must obey and stay inside," replied Rihani a little nervously.

Avery noticed that both Rihani and Ema shuddered. "They too are affected by the intense screams," he thought.

"Women are not allowed to go up onto the mountain, only the men can go. They hunt noddy birds and cut down the great tomano trees to make dugout canoes," explained Rihani.

"But we can go part way up to collect the pandanus fruit," continued Ema.

"W-what do spirits eat?" Avery asked suspiciously.

"Spirits? They do not eat anything," replied Rihani.

"So th-the spirits come down from the mountain to check on you and make sure you obey? Obey what?" asked Avery.

"Well, yes. We must obey our taboos and pray to our gods and ancestors. But the spirits also come down to the sea for cleansing," replied Rihani.

"Cleansing?" asked Avery, doubting what he was hearing.

"It is a cleansing wind that carries the spirits off the mountain and out to sea. The wind has power and can do that. The spirits will return to the mountain of course, because that is where they live," replied Rihani.

"What about rain? Doesn't rain cleanse the mountain?" asked Avery, even more mystified.

"The gods in the sky give us rain and feed the land so things will grow. But only the sea can heal and cleanse. When we are sick, we bathe in the sacred pool in the sea. When you wash a baby in the sea, the baby will cry. That is what happens to the mountain. The mountain is crying because it is being washed and cleansed by the spirits that live there."

"How do you know all this stuff?" said Avery. "The spirits cleansing the mountain?" He was sceptical and believing at the same time. Some things on this island were unexplainable.

"When the mountain cries, we know it is crying because it is being cleansed. But when the screams are angry, we know the spirits are angry with us or are warning us. Only our mother and the other sorcerers and sorceresses can speak to the spirits. One day, Ema and I will also speak to the spirits," replied Rihani proudly.

Avery was more than a bit confused and fearful too. He had never thought much about spirits or ghosts before. He had been in a church in London once, but he did not like it and got out. He heard tales about banshees and the Little People from some of the sailors, but such things were not for him. For Avery, religion and beliefs were for 'toffs'. Yet on this island, things were different. Things like the spirits, the ominous mountain, the smoke and the ability to 'read' the birds. "Hell!" he said. "I just don't know." Rihani was different too, he knew. Different and somehow special.

Finally, the day had come. Aio approached him early one morning. "Avery it is time."

"T-time?" asked Avery, although he suspected that his 'smoking' would be delayed no longer.

"You are now no longer weak. We must see if our gods accept you as one of us. Today, I will show you how to catch a noddy bird. You must care for this bird. If it dies, a black spirit resides in you and you must leave the island. We will also cover you with the black ink of the octopus and this will protect you. After ten days, you will kill the bird and Eigara will spill the blood over our sacred pinnacle. You will stay in your hut for three days and three nights and we will use the smoke of our sacred tree to ward away any evil spirit that still lingers in you. Once the three days are over, Eigara shall read the blood on the sacred pinnacle of our ancestors. If the gods have accepted you. You will remain here as one of us."

Avery felt frightened. He looked at Rihani who was standing near her hut. She smiled at him. Somehow this gave him courage. He could feel her gaze as he unwillingly followed her father to learn how to catch a noddy bird with a net attached to a long pole. This was something he had never done before and he was sure he would make a fool of himself. He did indeed have difficulties catching the bird, but with Aio's help, he finally managed it. The first step of his ritual was completed. Aio then put the bird in a small cage for Avery to carry.

He was taken to a special hut. Eigara and Rihani entered soon after. They painted his body with the black ink of the octopus. As they dipped their fingers in the ink, they chanted a strange invocation. The chant sent shivers up his spine. When they left he looked at the strange patterns they had designed all over his body. He knew he could leave his hut, but felt exhausted and so lay back down on his mat and slept. He dreamt of Rihani. She was in the form of a strange, silvery haze. He tried to follow her, but when he was in reach, she slipped further away. The next morning, he left his hut in search of Rihani. He found her but she looked away as if he were a stranger. He did not understand why. "She's avoiding me. She was my friend," he thought sadly. He felt alone and spent his days roaming the shoreline carrying the caged noddy bird.

On the tenth day, Avery was summoned. He was told to stand over the stone altar and kill the noddy bird. The blood was collected in a coconut shell. Avery's stomach lurched at the thought of killing his pet bird, as he had become rather attached to it. He wanted to refuse and free it, let it fly away, but he knew that it would be his life or the bird's.

Eigara, Rihani and Ema stood beside him and chanted. At first the chant was slow, but it slowly became louder and faster until he could feel the pounding of his heart. He took the small bird, closed his eyes and cut off its head, letting the blood drip into the bowl. He had never killed anything before. He felt sick and had to fight to keep the bile in his stomach. Perspiration was running down his body, leaving strange streaks as it ran into the black ink.

Avery thought he would break, he was so tense. Then he felt a soft hand touch his arm and he opened his eyes. Rihani stood there and motioned for him to follow her. He followed her into his hut and there in the centre a fire was burning. The hut was only lightly smoky and was surprisingly not unpleasant. He collapsed onto his mat and placed his hands into his face. He did not want to see anyone. He wanted to be alone. Eigara, still chanting, took the blood down to the sea. There she poured it over the sacred pinnacles and then left.

For three days Avery stayed in his hut. Food and water as well as dry leaves were left outside his hut. It was up to him to keep the fire going. His sleep was restless as he had to constantly put leaves on the fire to keep it smoking. He felt hot and dirty. He had not bathed since the day the ink was painted on his body. The streaks on his body reminded him of when he worked in the tanning factory. Somehow, he began to think about his time in London. "Maybe it wasn't that bad after all," he thought despondently.

Finally, one morning Gadiya came into his hut and told him to follow him to bathe in the sea. He noticed the people of the village standing around the stone altar. Eigara, Rihani and Ema were sitting cross-legged in front of the altar chanting. When he finished bathing, he was taken to the stone altar. He felt his heart beat in trepidation of what was to follow. His life now depended on what Eigara would say. He looked down at Rihani. She had her eyes closed and he felt a strange stirring within him. "I can't leave her," he thought as he too closed his eyes to the sound of the repeated monotone words of the chant. He started to relax, lulled by the chant that seemed endless. Avery was startled as Eigara voice broke into his consciousness. She was now standing in front of him.

"The gods have spoken. The evil spirit that lived within you has left. Our ancestors have accepted you. You may live on our island. You must obey our taboos, or you will be punished." She then turned and walked into her hut.

"It's over," thought Avery with overwhelming relief. He looked at Rihani and she beamed at him. She stood up and walked towards the sea. Avery quickly followed and together they strolled along the reef without speaking.

As the months passed, Avery could communicate fluently with the tribe. The people were curious and asked him many questions about where he came from. They would sit around the fire at night and listen to him talk about the far away land he had come from.

"Many people live in large villages called 'towns'. Larger villagers, like the one I came from, we call 'cities'. The 'cities' are so big and the buildings so high that the sun is hidden, and people live in the shadows. The air is not sweet like on this island, but always smells like sewage and filth. The sky is very rarely blue. It's mostly grey. At night you cannot see the stars, because everything is covered with a thick smoke. Some people have too much food and other things, whilst others die because they have nothing, not even enough to eat. So people fight and kill so they can survive. Here on your island, it's always warm. But where I came from it can be very, very cold, and people die because of this cold. Here, people do not kill each other for food or greed. You are very fortunate," Avery would often recount sadly. However, at times, almost unbelievably, he missed that old, familiar world.

Although the Islanders could not visualise many of the things Avery was describing, they were fascinated by his stories. For a long time, they had believed that they were the centre of the world. They were aware of the existence of some other islands, for over time a few canoes that were lost at sea had beached on their Island. But the stories told by Avery of distant lands populated by so many people were just incredible.

Avery often went fishing beyond the reef with Gadiya and Itu in their canoe. It was on one of these trips that they saw a ship on the horizon. Gadiya and Itu became afraid, for they thought it was a monstrous sea bird.

"It's not a bird. It's a large canoe called a 'ship'. But the men on the large canoe can be very dangerous," Avery informed the other two boys. He felt a strange sensation in his stomach as his past fears flooded back to him. He felt an acute depression and a sense of foreboding taking hold. "If they find me, they will take me back. They may even hang me for desertion," he thought.

The boys quickly paddled back to shore to find Aio and the elders of the tribe. They knew that they were in imminent danger, for they had been waiting for an evil spirit since before Avery's arrival. This monstrous canoe with its strange wings could be the vessel bringing the evil spirit with it. Eigara stood beside her husband and other members of the village as they watched on the distant horizon the large dark silhouette approaching their home. She slowly turned to her people and stated gravely, "The time has come." Then she turned around and went inside her hut where she sat and called to their ancestors for help.

Avery looked around and said, "It's a large canoe called a 'ship'. On board there are many men and they can be very dangerous. On some islands, men go ashore and trade for water, meat, fruit and fish, and they leave without causing harm. But on some ships, the men go on shore and kill the people living there." Avery shuddered. Perhaps this ship had come to take him back? He looked around to see where Rihani was, then went and stood beside her. She then surprised him by slipping her trembling hand into his. For the first time in his life he felt strong and protective of Rihani who always seem so spirited and proud.

That night chief Aio called a meeting.

"While these strange men are on our island, the women and children must hide in the caves. I will send messengers to the other tribes on the island to warn them to do the same."

"We should leave now!" cried the women.

"No, the reef is dangerous and will guard our village during the night. Tomorrow you will leave when the sun rises. Tonight, prepare food and water to take into the caves," Aio ordered.

That night the people of the village were too afraid to sleep. "These strangers may have powers that would allow them to pass through the reef and kill us in our sleep. Avery has told us stories of the wondrous powers of these men," they whispered to each other. Aio also felt distrustful. He stationed two men to stand watch. The moon was high and they could see if anyone approached the reef.

Rihani lay beside Ema in their hut. She had no doubts that the world they had known until now would change. "Dark spirits are arriving on our island." She trembled at the thought and her tears flowed. She saw again the imagines of her people dying on the shore. She had felt safe with Avery's hand holding hers, but now she was alone and her dream came back to her. She wanted to run from her hut and find him so she would not feel so afraid, but knew that she could not.

Early the next morning, the women and children packed their belongings and headed quickly up to the caves on the side of the dark mountain. There they met the women and children from some of the other villages. They hid in the limestone caves and anxiously waited until Aio would send a messenger to tell them they could return to their villages.

Eigara, Rihani and Ema, together with other sorceresses from the nearby villages, sat in a circle and called to their gods and ancestors to protect them. Eigara invoked her ancestors as she swayed backwards and forwards in time with her chant. Her ancestors were the most powerful on the island and only with their help would she know if their men would be safe. The sounds of the voices around her disappeared as she entered further and further into her trance. She could see the men gathered on the beach, but felt that they were in no imminent danger. Relieved she slowly withdrew from her trance-like state.

The captain of the Victoria sailed the whaling ship slowly towards the island. The sea was uncharted in this part of the world and the island itself was not shown on his map of the Pacific. From what Captain Fitzsimons Caines could see from his telescope, the island was small with a high towering mountain in the centre. It was lush with vegetation and he had seen fires along the coastline the night before, so he knew it was inhabited. Captain Caines was not too pleased to have to stop at another inhabited, uncharted island, but he needed fresh water and food. He hoped that the natives were friendly.

He could see that a dangerous reef surrounded the island, so gave orders to anchor the ship and lower two boats. They would have to row a long way in to shore. He knew that if they had to leave the island quickly, they would be exposed for a longer period of time due to their distance from the ship. Twelve members of the crew boarded the boats and rowed cautiously to the shoreline. The men were heavily armed. They knew that on some islands, the natives were hostile and there was always the risk that they could become food themselves.

Head Chief Aio and the other men of his tribe waited patiently on the beach. Other chiefs and members of the nearby villages also joined Aio. The chiefs all wore their finest adornments to show their power, and to ward off evil spirits in time of battle. Whale teeth were proudly worn by the chiefs. These were the most sought after of adornments, for they represented strong powers and only the chief of each tribe was permitted to wear them.

The natives felt confident that they could defeat any aggression by the strange men coming towards them in the large canoes. However, Avery had warned them that these men would carry guns. His explanation of a gun was not truly believed, but the men were very suspicious nevertheless. Avery had also explained about metal knives and bayonets, so although the men were confident that they far outnumbered the men coming ashore, they still felt apprehensive.

Once on shore, Captain Caines stood flanked by all but two of his men, who were ordered to wait near the boats. When he spotted Avery, he felt somewhat relieved. "If a white boy lives here with these natives they should not be dangerous, and maybe we can communicate better with them," he thought as he walked cautiously towards them.

Avery stood behind Aio and the other chiefs. He was still afraid these men would take him back. He had not completed his contract so was wary of the men. As soon as the captain and his men approached the tribe, Aio turned to Avery and nodded. Avery knew that he could not hide, but had to communicate between the two parties.

"Welcome to our island," he said, translating Aio's words to the captain.

"We come in peace," replied the captain.

"Why have you come?" asked Aio, and Avery

translated.

"We need fresh water and food for our ship. We can exchange great gifts for your food." The captain looked around suspiciously. There were about two hundred men on the beach, but no women or children.

"We will give you food. What gifts have you brought us?" asked Aio. The captain then ordered two of the men to fetch the hatchets, knives, mirrors, beads, tobacco and two guns from the boats. He demonstrated to Aio and the natives the power of the rifles. This was also a way of showing them their superior power. He lifted the loaded gun and pointed it to an overflying bird and then pulled the trigger. The noise itself frightened the natives, and when they picked up the dead bird they were awestruck at the magic of this new weapon.

The Islanders looked in amazement at the other goods to be exchanged, for they had never seen such wondrous things before. Aio and the other chiefs were pleased, so they began to barter for the goods. A pig was worth a hatchet, and then there were chickens, coconuts, taro and pandanus fruit. Most exciting of all to the Islanders were the guns, which were exchanged for dried coconut flesh called copra. The Islanders had learnt to dry coconut flesh and stored it to use in times of drought which happened every few years. Once the bartering was completed, the first load of food was brought forward and loaded onto the boats.

The exchange had taken all day. When the sun was beginning to set, the captain and crew returned to their ship with the plan to revisit the island on the following day. The Islanders were friendly, but experience had taught Captain Caines sailors who stayed onshore could be killed during the night, leaving the natives to keep both the goods and food.

In all, the exchange took two days to complete. Water was carried from the brackish ponds and emptied into the ship's barrels. Cages for the pigs and chickens were built and the fruit and vegetables were stored in large crates. Finally, the captain was well pleased with his reception and the exchange of goods and pulled the Victoria back out to sea. He made a note in the Captain's logbook: "The island looks small. A mountain lays at the centre of the island, probably an old volcanic crater. Because of the low-lying clouds, we could not determine how high the mountain actually was. A dangerous reef surrounds the island. About two hundred men participated in the exchange. No women or children were in sight. An English boy was seen living with the natives. His name and circumstances remain unknown. The boy, however, helped facilitate the trade as he could speak the native tongue. The natives were very friendly but naive. They were astounded by our superior goods and were more than willing to exchange these for food and water. I have named the island Volcano Island."

Aio and the rest of the Islanders watched the ship disappear into the horizon. Then he turned to the men. "We have many new things that will help us. The hatchets and steel knives cut better than our clam axes. The guns are very powerful. If more of these strange men return and attack us, we will defend ourselves better. I am happy with the exchange, but I am glad these men have left our island. It is time to call our women and children home, and for all tribes to return to their own villages."

Rihani, Ema and the rest of the women anxiously returned to their villages. They were curious about the arrival of the men on the big canoe with the large white wings. That night there was a great celebration. A large pig was killed and cooked in an underground oven. Taro, sago and other vegetables were wrapped in coconut leaves and placed over the pig to be cooked as well. Everyone was happy. There was singing and dancing all night. The men happily chewed the bitter tasting tobacco that was given to them by the men from the large canoe. Avery, however, did not join in the celebration but sat alone on the reef. He felt a deep sense of foreboding.

Chapter Ten
The Guardian

Avery stood in front of a cave high up on the mountain. Aio had accompanied him part of way and then left him there alone. Avery looked at the dark entrance and felt the fine hair on his body stand on end. He trembled and cautiously looked around. The surrounding undergrowth looked menacing. He could feel something or someone watching him.

"Aio are you still here?" he called. Nobody answered. "I'm stupid, there's nothing here. It's this island. I-it's just my imagination. I don't understand these people and their spirits! Spirits don't exist. My ancestors don't exist. B-but what if there is some truth in this? What then? What can I do? Nah!" he growled angrily. He felt tired, thirsty, angry, depressed and alone.

He looked warily into the dark cave, but could not bring himself to enter it. "I could just wait for a few days in a clearing and pretend I was finding my guardian," he sighed. "What do you want from me?" he yelled to the unseen eyes. He listened, hoping someone or something would give him an answer but only an eerie silence surrounded him. He let himself sink to the ground, feeling morose. He did not want to think or move and he let his self-pity overwhelm him. His heart quaked as a high-pitched scream tore through the undergrowth. Without thinking, he jolted up and scrambled into the cave. He hid behind a protruding rock and closed his eyes.

"Oh God! What have I gotten into? At least back in London and on the ship I only had to deal with men. Here,

I don't know! How can I escape?" His hands covered his face as he slid down onto the rough ground. Then slowly, without warning, the tears started. They kept flowing in an unending stream. He cried and cried. He could not remember if he had ever cried before. The sensation was unfamiliar. At one point, he tried to open his eyes but could not. They had swollen shut.

He felt thirsty. So thirsty. He reached into the woven satchel he carried and felt for the large coconut containing the potion Eigara had given him. He did not want to drink potions. He wanted water, but he felt so parched and thirsty. He pulled out the potion and cautiously sipped it. It tasted thick, gritty and bitter.

"What can I do?" he thought. The words of the chant Eigara had taught him flowed over and over in his mind, until he whispered the words aloud. His body started to mechanically rock backwards and forwards, but like when he was a child and in pain, nobody came to help him. He was alone. Always alone.

His chanting became louder and louder. Strange images appeared around him. His eyes were still swollen and so watery that he could barely make out the translucent, shimmering apparitions that were walking around, ignoring him. Then the vision became clearer. He saw a small boy in a workhouse, rocking backwards and forwards. The child was shivering from the cold bitter winter and his stomach ached from the hunger cramps. The vision changed and he watched, horrified, as he saw the boy cower in front of an ugly, black, deformed shadow that was beating him. The pain was unbearable as the cane pounded onto his fragile body. He was so small, defenceless and terrified. He rocked back and forwards. Avery screamed angrily. He hated this man and wanted to kill him!

He looked down at his hands. He was holding some strange, dark forms. They were souls. "I didn't know we could see souls," he fleetingly thought. He looked deeper at the dark, empty souls and shuddered. They started to evaporate. For how long he sat there and watched the hazy images float around him, he did not know. He felt around for the potion and took another drink. His body felt unreal. It was so light that he started floating up and up, until he could see the limestone ceiling of the cave. Then he started floating outside. All around he could see a mist. It lifted him higher and higher. The joy of this freedom was overwhelming and felt the tears flowing again. Through the hazy images of his tears, he could see a strange tree below. It stood out amongst the others. Its dry branches reached up, welcoming him, like a mother receiving her child to be embraced. He gently floated to the ground.

Avery rubbed his eyes, confused, and looked around. He was back in the cave. His head was throbbing. "What did Eigara give me?" he asked aloud. There was no answer. Exhausted he laid down and fell into a deep sleep. The warmth of the sun gently stroked him awake. Slowly he sat up and looked around, mystified. He was at the foot of the tree. The trunk was larger than he remembered and the dry branches now had small green buds. He felt thirsty and sipped the liquid from the coconut, gagging at the bitterness. A strange, cold vapour engulfed him and he started trembling. He could smell putrid skins rotting. "Where am I?" he murmured.

A heart-wrenching wail filled the cave as the unexpected pain of a leather strap lashed into his back. A monstrous hand retracted the whip for the third time as he turned and glared into the angry eyes of the perpetrator. He hated this vile master and felt a strong urge to kill him. He looked closer. The man's eyes were missing and only empty sockets remained. The image slowly evaporated.

Avery opened his eyes and looked around. A warm mist surrounded him. There was a large shadow in front of him. He stood up and staggered blindly, gravitating towards the silhouette. The mist parted. The tree welcomed him again. It appeared larger, stronger, and more vibrant. The images swirled around him, becoming darker and darker. Thick, black, sticky tentacles were pulling him deeper and deeper into a monstrous pit where grotesque hands were reaching up for him. The pit smelled rancid, like on board the whaling ship. He gagged.

The whaling ship was floating around and around the black, murky substance of the pit. He could make out the crew, swearing, drinking, fighting. The familiar fear was still deep within him. He hated these men and wanted them to drown in the putrid liquid of the pit. He felt himself sinking down further towards the vortex. The hands touching him were slimy and putrid. From a distance he could hear unfamiliar words. They comforted him and he murmured them repeatedly until they become a chant. As the chant became louder and louder, the hands slowly retracted and the dark tentacles faded. His body was able to float up from the abyss. The bright sun and colours of the island flashed across his mind. They overwhelmed the dark images of his nightmares.

"Rihani!" he called tentatively. The thought of her seemed to comfort him. He thought of Ema, Gudiya, Itu. He smiled, remembering the clear blue water as he fished with his friends. Here on this island, the people were his friends. He had never had friends before.

"Rihani," he whispered again. He could see her smiling and laughing. Then the image changed. He saw Rihani's face superimposed over Eigara's and shivered. He respected Eigara, but there was something different and frightening about her.

"Rihani is her mother," he murmured as he drifted into a deep dreamless sleep. The next morning he looked around, confused. He took out the potion Eigara gave him and drank the last of the remaining liquid. He began the now familiar chant.

Avery stood before the tree. Sunlight shone through the bright green leaves. He stood motionless unable to move. The beauty of the place was magnetic. He looked around and could feel a presence. This time he felt no fear. The presence felt safe.

"Who are you?" he asked, but he could only hear the breeze stirring the leaves of the tree.

"I know you're here. Please talk to me," he said.

Nothing moved. Not a stir. The rustling of the leaves had also stopped.

"Are you my ancestor?" he asked.

Still there was no reply. Then from far away, he could hear the mountain. It was a soft, strange sound. For the first time since arriving on the island, the mountain cries did not frighten him. Avery closed his eyes and continued chanting the sacred words. When he woke up, he was back in the cave.

"Did I dream about the tree? It was so real," he whispered to the creatures he could sense scurrying around the cave walls and floor. He did not know how long he spent in the cave. Everything seemed like a dream, yet it was so real.

Avery slowly got up from where he had been sitting just inside the cave, behind the protruding rock. He looked around and sighed.

"I must find Rihani," he murmured.

He slowly walked down from the mountain, feeling at peace, and entered the village. He saw Rihani sitting beside her sister and approached them. Rihani felt his presence and ran towards him. They stood in front of each other and smiled shyly. Then they started laughing.

Chapter Eleven
Convicts

Old ship hulk used as prison

Liam Petterson sat looking down at the remains of the body and felt nauseated. Together with the other five members on the boat, he had just cannibalised one of their group who had died that same day. None of the other escapees dared ask how his death had occurred. Life had always been difficult for Liam, as it had been for the other men who shared the boat with him. He was born in one of the small, windowless rooms on the dirty, overcrowded streets of London. As far as he knew he was the only surviving child in his family. His parents were often drunk and would take out their desperation and anger on him, as if he were the cause of their problems. His father, like many others, rarely found work, and what money he did earn, he used to buy cheap alcohol. His mother worked most nights, selling the only thing she had: herself.

How he had survived those first five years was a miracle in itself, as very few children did. Violent parents often killed their small children through abuse or neglect. Liam knew that he had had other brothers or sisters, for he remembered hearing the screams from his mother in labour and the faint cries of newborn babies. They lived in one room and he was familiar with many ugly and painful things. He remembered the bloodied bundles being hurried out of the room. They were never mentioned by his parents and he knew better than to ask questions. He was only five when he ran away from that dark, dank room after yet another vicious beating. That had been the last time that he cried.

Liam gave up his battle to hold down the raw flesh he had just consumed, and leaned over the side of the boat to regurgitate all of his stomach contents. He held on as the fierce cramps gripped him and looked at the other five remaining men. They too looked uneasy and looked away. He knew he had done many contemptible things in his life, but he had finally reached the lowest point of all. He had put the flesh of another human in his mouth. The cramps finally subsided and Liam let his mind wander, remembering the past. There was nothing else to do but remember.

When he ran away from his parents, he joined a group of

boys of various ages and they taught him how to steal. As he grew more proficient, he became better at it and also more ruthless. He smiled to himself, remembering those years on the street. He had become adept at stealing and so did not go hungry. There were always the taverns at night and he often drank with girls who worked there. But he had become cocky and careless and was captured and sentenced to one of the dreaded 'prison hulks'. He shuddered at the memory.

In his mind, he could see again the dreaded hulk. It was an old ship transformed into a floating prison. Prison hulks were notorious and very few of their inmates came out alive from that hell. It was a way of eliminating unwanted prisoners in the overflowing prison system. Everyone, including the authorities and prisoners themselves, knew that the squalid living conditions and brutality of the other desperate prisoners meant that those who were sent to these hulks had little chance of surviving their sentences. Liam shuddered again. He could still visualise the old, rotting ship. The hulk could only contain three hundred prisoners. However, they were always overcrowded and far exceeded that number. The hulk he was sent to was, he felt, one of the more deplorable examples. It had three decks: upper, middle and lower. Prisoners who were deemed the worst criminals were kept on the lower deck. The idea was that as they redeemed their characters and served their sentences, they could progress to the next deck. However, the prisoners sentenced to the lower deck rarely survived. There was no air circulating down there and the floors were layered with faeces. Liam could smell the lower deck from where he lay on the second deck, not that it was much better.

Like all prisoners, he was always kept in irons. Some had irons on only one leg while others had them on both. Not that anyone could move anyway. He remembered he could barely turn and movement was never an option. Once a day, he was fed bread and water. The bread was often stale and infested with worms. He was supposed to have been issued clothing and a blanket, but most authorities did not comply with government guidelines and kept these allowances for themselves. Liam wore only the rags in which he had when he was caught, together with an old tattered blanket he had taken from a dead prisoner. He was lucky, he thought to himself, even though he was sentenced to the middle deck. The prisoners were fed poorly, and the stronger and more vicious convicts would forcibly take the food from the weaker ones. Prisoners were often so hungry that any rats that were caught would be eaten raw. They were considered a delicacy and prisoners would kill each other to get hold of one.

In summer the hulks were sweltering hot and in winter they were freezing. There were no portholes, so fresh air could not enter the decks, and the men, in desperation, often fought amongst themselves and were killed. Some of the more fortunate prisoners on the upper deck were allowed to go above to clean the ship, so they at least got some fresh air occasionally. The smell of the hulk was tangible even far inland. Men on the upper deck were sometimes recruited into the navy when their sentences were almost complete.

Liam worked his way up from the middle deck onto the upper deck. He could sometimes could go above and help clean. It was whilst he was prisoned on the upper deck that he met Owen and Briggs. Then one day his name was read from a list. Liam remembered how relieved he was to hear that, together with Owen and Briggs, he would be transported to a prison colony. Liam did not care where this colony was. All that mattered was that he had survived the dreaded hulk.

He remembered boarding the Nexus thinking that he and his companions were the lucky ones. On board the ship, however, they were chained below deck and life was not much better than the hulk. As the voyage progressed, the prisoners started getting bored and restless. The prison colony was far away and their fate there was unknown. Hence, the more daring prisoners, together with some of the corrupt crew members who had once also been prisoners, secretly contrived to take over the ship. They thought it would be a chance for them to achieve freedom and thus a plot was hatched.

Mutiny had been relatively easy. Liam smiled again to himself, remembering how it had happened. The captain, first mate and other sailors were killed in their sleep and thrown overboard. That night however, whilst the freed prisoners and the mutinous crew were getting drunk, Liam, Owen and Briggs, together with another three men, lowered a boat full of provisions, guns and gin into the sea. They had decided they would take their chances on one of the islands that dotted the Pacific, rather than risk being caught again and hanged.

Liam sighed. For the first two weeks, they had plenty to eat and drink. The men were happy to be free and optimistic that they would soon spot an island. But as the days became weeks and the food became scarcer, everyone grew more apprehensive. No island had yet been spotted, and they thought that they would have landed somewhere by now. The vast Pacific Ocean had also proved unpredictable. Storms had battered the boat ruthlessly, but somehow they still managed to stay afloat. The confined quarters on board the boat had become dangerous. The food had run out and there was only gin to drink. A sense of dread shrouded the boat and tempers were at boiling point. Violent arguments started breaking out. Given the drunken state of the men, these arguments became more vicious as the days dragged on. All those on the boat realised that if they did not find food and water soon, they would perish. The gin only made them thirstier, so they were reluctant to drink larger quantities. They started becoming suspicious of each other and each felt uneasy. Liam remembered taking turns keeping watch with Owen and Briggs; they did not trust the other men. Then this morning one of their shipmates was found dead. Nobody asked any questions. They were so hungry and desperate that it had been decided they would cut the body up and eat it. He was dead anyhow, and if they did not eat, they too would soon all die.

After emptying the contents of his stomach overboard, Liam found his hunger had now resurfaced. Slowly he cut another piece of flesh from the body. For the moment the remaining five men were saved from starvation and the raw meat had also quenched their thirst. But the body had to be eaten quickly, as the tropical heat had quickly deteriorated it. When hunger and thirst set in again, the men once again became fearful of one another. They became even more suspicious, knowing that they too could be killed and eaten by the others. So, they slept very little and this lead to more fights. One such fight became so vicious that another member on the boat was killed and he too was eaten.

The surviving men had now become even more wary. Owen, Liam and Briggs whispered amongst themselves. They planned to kill the fourth occupant of the canoe, and so one night the three men attacked the remaining occupant and killed him too. Now, each of the three survivors realised that it was only a matter of time before one of them would also be sacrificed. At this point, Liam realised he had to survive for only the most ruthless had a chance. He also realised that he had reached the lowest point of human depravation, for he too would kill and eat one of his comrades in order to survive.

As the sun started to rise, Liam gazed wearily in the horizon. He rubbed his dry, sore eyes in order to focus them better. Out in the distance, he thought he could see the outline of a distant island. At first he did not believe it. "Maybe it's only a low lying cloud," he thought to himself. But the more he gazed at the distant shadow, the more he was convinced it was land.

"Wake up!" he yelled.

The other two men jumped up, startled. He pointed to the distant horizon and they too yelled. They felt that their luck had finally changed. They knew that the inhabitants on some islands were hostile, but they had guns and so had the superior power to subdue the natives, if there were any problems.

Chapter Twelve
Beachcombers

Aio was awakened just before dawn.

"AIO! AIO!" shouted a messenger outside the Head Chief's hut.

Aio woke up, startled. Eigara was still sleeping on her mat beside him. He got up quickly and went outside. There was Irumi, a man from another tribe who lived on the other side of the island. Aio felt tense as he knew something was wrong, but he had to stay calm for he was the Head Chief. He nodded to Irumi in acknowledgement, and waited patiently to hear what was so important that the man had come so early to seek him out.

"There are strange men along the beach down from our village. They are like the ones that came in the big canoe," Irumi stated breathlessly. He had been running all night, ever since two men from his clan had noticed the fire down by the beach and his chief had sent him to inform Aio.

Irumi belonged to the Iwa clan. Their village was not situated along the beach like the other villages around the island, but was settled around a small inland lake. However, that night two of the men were hunting noddy birds with their nets, and they had noticed a fire along the shoreline. They quietly approached the fire and noticed the three strange men.

Aio, thought for a while and stated, "We will not approach these men, but we must keep watch to see if they bring us danger. Go back to your tribe and spread the message to the other tribes on the island. They may not mean us any harm, but we must be vigilant."

Aio then entered his hut and sat down on his mat, thinking of what may lie ahead with the arrival of these strange, pale men. He knew that Eigara would help him understand, so would wait until she woke up to ask. When Eigara woke up, she was surprised to see her husband sitting there watching her. "You are awake early," she smiled.

"I have had a message from the Iwa clan. Three pale men like those on the big canoe are on the island. I have sent messengers to the other clans living on the island. We will do nothing until these men approach us." Aio looked serious. "What if I am mistaken?" he thought. "Do the spirits tell us these men mean us harm? Was that the warning we had from the spirits of the mountains?" Aio looked uncertainly at his wife.

Eigara looked sadly at her husband and quietly replied, "I do not know. The spirits only warned us that we are in great danger and there will be a time of great sorrow."

Something on the island changed subtly. Rihani could not see any change, but deep inside she felt uneasy. She no longer went out of her hut at night. The dark undergrowth surrounding the village looked dangerous and she could not shake the feeling of being watched. The island had always been safe. Children could wander around unaccompanied at any time of the day or night. Now a strange uneasiness seemed to settle on the island. The Islanders did not speak about it, but the children were now more carefully guarded. Aio also felt this angst. It was for this reason that the men on the beach were closely watched.

The beachcombers seem to keep to themselves and made

no attempt to approach the Islanders. The men shot birds to eat and collected coconuts that had fallen from the high trees. Aio, after some time gave orders for the tribes to ignore them, but he still felt disturbed about the unwanted presence. Eigara, together with Rihani and Ema, would often sit inside Eigara's hut and sing the chants invoking the spirits of their ancestors. They also left offerings of food and flowers more often at the altar. The Islanders felt uneasy with strangers on their island and Eigara's predictions still loomed on their minds.

Rihani and Avery met often. However, as time passed their meeting were sometimes a little volatile. On some occasions, they would be laughing, and yet at other times they became angry without any apparent reason. Neither understood the strange emotions each had towards one another. One day Rihani wanted to be alone. She was walking along the reef when she came across a dead fish. She knelt down and looked closely at it. The fish had been savaged and its stomach had been ripped out of it. She held her breath. The fish was a sign. It was a sign of violence and death. Tears ran down her face for she knew that the violence was directed at her. Frightened, she ran in search of her mother.

"Mother, please come and look," she requested breathlessly.

Eigara followed her daughter along the shore until they came to the dead fish. Eigara felt a sharp pain and trembled. She started to chant and looked away into the distance.

"Mother. It is a sign of violence, is it not?"

Eigara looked at her daughter and nodded.

"I found the fish, so the violence will involve me." Rihani shivered and looked expectantly at her mother. Perhaps she was mistaken. However, her mother nodded and continued her chant. She had to invoke her ancestors to help protect Rihani, for she feared for her daughter's life.

A few more weeks passed and the Islanders started noticing that food was vanishing from the villages. Chickens and vegetables kept mysteriously disappearing. Then two young girls also disappeared. The clans started accusing one another of these thefts, so a meeting of the chiefs was called. That night, the men sat around the fire and discussed the disappearance of the young girls and the food.

"Iwi has gone!" shouted chief Erani from the Kalab clan.

"Kabaya has also disappeared!" shouted chief Dara from the Yarle clan.

"We have lost many chickens and a piglet!" shouted some of the men.

"We have lost taro, yams and chickens!" yelled other men sitting around the fire.

Aio sat and listened whilst the men accused each other of stealing. It would not have been the first time that clans had stolen from each other, but never in such quantities and never before had young girls also disappeared.

"Did Iwi or Kabaya go out on the reef to fish?" asked Aio.

"No, Iwi went to fetch water from the pond," shouted chief Erani.

"And Kabaya was gathering taro," shouted chief Dara.

"The girls could have been taken by the spirit world as a sacrifice," stated other members of the clans seriously.

"The spirits have never taken young girls as sacrifices before. I shall ask Eigara. We need to keep vigilant. Do not let the women fetch water or go out of the villages by themselves," ordered Aio.

The men sat around the fire until late that night. Those who had come from other villages around the island lay down their mats and went to sleep near the fire. They would return to their villages the following morning and notify their tribes of what Aio had ordered. The beachcombers also sat around their fire along the shoreline. They were satisfied with their island, for there was food and girls for the taking.

"Whot if tha natives find we took tha gels?" asked Liam.

"Who cares? We 'ave tha guns!" laughed Owen and Briggs.

"Maybe, shouldn't 'ave killed dat native we met on the track," Liam commented as an afterthought.

"Coodna lef him, cood we? Seen us, 'e did, with tha food, didn't 'e?" replied Briggs.

"Whot ye worried about anyway? We 'ave tha guns!" sniggered Owen.

Liam nodded in agreement, though the mountain screams were getting on his nerves. "No use worrying. They're right," thought Liam as he had another drink.

"They're only a bunch o' savages!" laughed Owen again.

A grey, translucent mist swirled around the shoreline and a high-pitched scream followed by a low murmur came down from the mountain. The men shuddered and then laughed at their own foolishness.

"It's just tha wind," they thought to themselves.

The haunting murmur weaved its way around the

men sitting on the beach and a cold chill embraced their bodies.

Chapter Thirteen
The Cave

After another restless night, Rihani awoke early. Ever since the fire in the sky, her dreams were strange and frightening. Unable to fall asleep again, she left the village to fetch clean water at the brackish ponds, unaware that Aio had given the order for women not to leave the village. She was kneeling down, filling her coconut shells at the ponds, when felt a rough hand cover her mouth. Her head whipped back violently. She tried to scream and pull the hand away from her mouth, but felt a painful blow to the side of the head. The last thing she saw was a red flash, and then nothing.

Rihani came to from her state of semi-consciousness and felt herself being carried. She felt the wet, sticky body of a man carrying her. It was not one of the men from the island. This man had a strong, acrid smell. The beachcombers carried her to a cave up on the side of the mountain. She was slung over a man's shoulder and her head kept bumping against his back. Each time it hit the sweaty, acrid body, her pain and nausea increased. The pain in her head was unbearable. Fortunately, when it increased to an intolerable level it suddenly stopped as she felt herself drift into the soothing, dark world of unconsciousness.

Some time later, Rihani slowly became aware of her surroundings. She felt stunned and confused, and her hands and feet were tightly bound. "Where am I? What happened?" she thought. She slowly lifted her head an inch from the sandy floor, opened her eyes and looked around, bewildered. It was cold and black and a strange coldness penetrated her body. The pain in her head was excruciating. She tried to sit up but felt dizzy. A wave of nausea made her lean over and throw up what little food had remained in her stomach from the morning's hurried meal.

Rihani closed her eyes and let the darkness take her once again. Sometime later, she tried to reopen them. Her body was trembling uncontrollable. Her mind called out to her mother, but she knew she was alone. She wanted to scream out for help, but instinctively knew she should not. Darkness surrounded her but she could sense eyes gazing at her. She was an intruder here. She could feel the phantoms and spirits of the dead. She was terrified. The small pouch around her neck containing the totems of tooth, root and bone had been lost and could no longer protect her. Danger was everywhere in the blackness that surrounded her. Her body was now hot and perspiring. No longer did she feel cold, but instead a fire was burning her body.

"Hurry! Run! Escape!" said a distant whisper.

Slowly, she tried again to ease herself up into a sitting position. She could feel the rough side of the cave and leaned back onto the cool rocks and closed her eyes to see if the dizziness would pass. The excruciating pain still pounded in her head.

"Hurry! Run! Escape!" She heard the whisper again.

Tentatively, she tried to open her eyes again. She felt a wave of nausea so closed them. Her head was still pounding.

"Hurry! Run! Escape!" Again she heard the distant echo.

Her throat was parched and she felt the unshed tears ready to stream down her face, but instinctively knew she had to be strong or would die.

"Hurry! Run! Escape!" the faint whisper kept urging her.

She opened her eyes once more and felt less nauseous. She began to make out the darker silhouettes of the rocks. In the distance, she could see a faint light and stared at it, trying not to blink so she could focus better. It looked like the entrance of a cave, and there were shadows of men sitting near a small fire. These were not her people. She could tell by their strange silhouettes. Every now and again, a high-pitched laugh made the hair on her body stand up. She could hear the men murmuring, but could not understand what they were saying. She could make out that they were drinking and her parched throat burnt even more.

"It may be better if the spirit world takes me. These men will make me suffer horrific pain. They will defile me and then kill me. I have not the strength to run. And run to where?" she thought desperately. She closed her eyes and called out to the spirit world to come and take her. Within moments, she felt a deep sleep-like trance embrace her.

Rihani stood up and looked at the body leaning against the cave wall below. She felt confused. What was she doing, sitting there with her head against the wall? She felt mystified at what she was seeing. "How can I be down there as well as standing here?" she asked herself.

Confused, she decided to ask the men at the entrance of the cave if they could explain what was happening to her, so she walked through the tunnel until she reached them.

She approached them without fear and asked, "Who are you? I have never seen you on our island before."

The strange men ignored her. It was not the custom of her people to be so poorly mannered. "People who come from the other world outside our island have very bad manners," she thought. Rihani took a final disgusted look at the three men who were drinking and laughing, and left the cave without uttering another word.

She started walking down the mountain, finding that felt very strange. She was so light she was almost floating! The rough ground beneath her feet was soft and the low murmur of the mountain spirits surrounded her as she glided through the undergrowth of the thick forest. Suddenly, she found herself entering her village. "My family must be worried," she thought. She could see her people gathered around a fire at in the centre of the village. They were angry and yelling. Ema was next to Avery and she was crying. Itu was standing alongside Gadiya and Adera. Like the rest of her clan, he was yelling at her father.

"Why are they yelling at my father?" she asked one of the women closest to her. The woman ignored her, so Rihani touched her shoulder to get her attention, but her hand could not feel anything. Terrified, she cried out, "Mother, Father, help me!" but nobody replied. Instead, everyone kept arguing. Rihani stood there frozen. "What is happening? Am I dreaming?" she asked herself.

"We must attack!" yelled some of the men from her village. "They have taken Rihani!"

"They have also desecrated an altar in the Iwa village and killed chief Daro. That is TABOO!" shouted the people.

"It is taboo to kill any person, much less a chief. Those

who have violated our customs must die!" yelled the men. The other members of the clans nodded in agreement.

"We do not know where these pale men have taken Rihani and the other girls. If we kill them we may never find them!" Aio yelled back.

Aio looked at Eigara. She was also crying for her daughter and the other two girls. Eigara then stood up and staggered to the stone altar. She lifted her arms to the sky and started whispering incomprehensible words, and then she started chanting. First it was a painful lament, but as the chant continued, it became more and more powerful. Eigara started swaying faster and faster until her body trembled uncontrollably. Only the whites of her eyes could be seen and her face became distorted in violent anger. Her chant now was becoming a scream. It sounded like the scream from the mountain spirits. Her words were lost and only the high-pitched, agonising, angry scream was audible.

Aio had never seen his wife look so angry, or perform this ritual before. He felt the skin on his body grow cold and he shivered at the intensity of the ritual. His wife was performing black magic! The clan looked at Eigara in fear and awe. They knew the men who had taken Rihani and the other girls would soon join their ancestors.

"I am here!" yelled Rihani, but she already understood that they would not answer her. They could not hear her.

Rihani looked around desperately, but she could do nothing. Maybe she had died in that cave and now she too had become a spirit? She looked away from her people, who were now prostrated on the ground around her mother, and peered down along the shoreline. She could see a girl sitting on a limestone bench. It was a little way from the beach and hidden from view by the overhead canopy. "I have lived here all my life and yet I have never noticed that nook," she thought.

Rihani walked towards the young girl. She was about the same age as herself, and yet she had never seen this girl on the island before. When she reached the girl, she noticed that she was crying. Rihani sat down beside her and placed her arm around her shoulders to comfort her. The girl looked up and smiled sadly at her.

"Why are you crying?" Rihani asked.

But the girl just lowered her head and wept louder. Her sobbing was agonising. Clearly, the girl was in great pain. "Please do not cry. I will help you," said Rihani. Tears were now also flowing from her own eyes.

"Yes, you will, but many of our people will die," the girl replied sadly.

Rihani looked more carefully at her. She was a lot smaller than herself, but looked vaguely familiar. Around her neck, she wore a beautiful shell necklace. Rihani was sure she recognised it. She had seen it in a small, woven basket inside her mother's hut. On the girl's face were the sacred tattoos that indicated she was a sorceress. They were the same tattoos Rihani's mother had.

"You must find it. It is in the cave. You must help our people." With these words, the girl stood up and walked slowly away.

Rihani felt the throbbing pain in her head return. She opened her eyes, bewildered. She was back in the cave, in her own body and she could see the silhouettes of three men still sitting at the entrance.

"I must have been dreaming," she shivered.

She tried to stand up, but her legs were too weak, and after a few attempts she gave up. She was in grave danger. Of this she was certain. Rihani thought about the girl on the beach and tried very hard to remember what she had told her. Something was in the cave, but what? "How am I to find something when I do not know what I am looking for? And how am I to find anything if I am tied up and cannot move?" she thought dejectedly. Then her thoughts turned to her mother. She could hear her voice saying, "Rihani, magic is in you. Mana is all around you, in the sky, the sea, the animals, the earth, the rocks. All things hold great power. You are a sorceress and you can call upon these powers to help you in times of need. The powerful mana of the things that surround you can be yours. You must believe in the power within you, the power given to you by our ancestors."

Rihani looked around again, but all she could see were dark shadows. She was overcome by fear. "Maybe this is where the spirits of the mountain live? Or it may be where the great, ancient spider that created the world and our ancestors live. Maybe that is what I am to find?" She shuddered, for she was afraid of spiders. "But what can I do? If I stay here, I am sure these men will kill me." Then she started thinking about her family. "They will suffer if I am killed. I am a sorceress like my mother and her mother before her. I am a sorceress and I have great powers in my blood. Ekewane is my powerful ancestor and she also lived in a time of great suffering. I will call to her for courage and I will escape and help my people. I am a sorceress! I am a sorceress!"

Then slowly she bowed her head and started whispering

the chant her mother had taught her. Her body rocked backwards and forwards as the words sounded in her head. The pounding of her heart grew faster and faster. At first, all she could hear was the thump, thump, thump of her heartbeat. Then slowly she withdrew from the thundering of her heart and listened. She could hear noises around her: the murmuring of the trees outside; the faint breeze coming through the cave entrance and winding its way down the tunnel through the jagged rocks on the sides; the small insects and spiders scurrying along on the cave floor and behind the coarse rocks on the floor and walls.

Rihani could feel her body reaching out and absorbing the unseen mana from within the cave. The power entered her stomach. "Magical power starts from your stomach," her mother had told her. She continued whispering the words of the chant. "The power within must come out through your voice," her mother had explained. Rihani whispered softly and her voice sounded like the breeze swirling around the tunnels. She continued to call out to Ekewane, her favourite ancestor, to give her strength and courage. After a while she opened her eyes again and no longer felt the paralysing fear. She felt stronger and knew that she must hide. She started crawling silently further back into the tunnel and away from the entrance of the cave.

Rihani felt the sharp rocks on the cave floor scratch and cut her arms and legs as she dragged herself along. Hot, sticky blood was trickling from the cuts and her perspiration was stinging them, but the pain felt subtle and distant. She tried not to think of what lay ahead and continued to crawl deeper into the mountain. For how long she kept crawling, she did not know. Her body felt tired and the pain in her head was now coming back stronger than before, but she kept going further and further into the darkness. Her only thought was to get as far away as possible from the men who had abducted her and to hide from them.

At one point, her tunnel came to larger opening. She felt her way around the space and discovered a second tunnel that turned left. She hesitated for a few moments and then decided to follow it. All night Rihani crawled along the floor of the cave. At one point, she was so tired she decided to have a few moments rest, but fell into an exhausted sleep. Once more, Rihani found herself standing in her village. The men were preparing for war. They were going to attack the beachcombers. Aio sat surrounded in a circle by the men of his tribe and the chiefs and men of the other tribes that lived on the island. He was angry. Rihani had disappeared and most likely be dead. The other two young girls missing from the villages had been discovered in-between the jagged pinnacles along the shoreline. They had been violated and murdered. The women on the island were now even more fearful to leave their huts. Rihani looked sadly at the men of the island and knew that many could die before the moon had gone to sleep and the sun had risen. The Islanders had only two guns and the pale men would have many. She wept for the killings that would happen and looked again at her father, and at Gadiya, her brother, and his friend Itu. Avery was also there. His months on the island had changed the colour of his skin. No longer pale, he had turned a light golden brown and was not the same colour as the intruders on their island. Nor was he now small and sickly. During his time on their island, he had grown and now his body was well formed and muscled. Rihani felt a deep connection to this boy she helped save and who had become a member of her clan.

Rihani opened her eyes. She was back in the cave. For a few moments, she wondered whether this was the dream. Everything felt surreal and confusing. But the pain in her body made the reality sink in. She felt fearful and desperate again. She was only a young girl and could not do much to save her people. "If I can do nothing for my people, I must at least show my family that I am still alive," she whispered to the silent cave dwellers.

Although her words were brave, she was exhausted and thirsty. She could not stop the tears of desperation running down her face. For how long she cried, she did not know, but after some time the tears ran out and she made up her mind that she would go no further into the cave. "I will not have the strength to return if I go on. I may get lost and not find my way back to the entrance," she thought. She hoped that by now the men had realised that she was gone and would not look for her this far into the cave. She hoped they had given up and gone away.

Rihani was not certain that the men had left and knew she had to be cautious. She sat there and listened for any noises to warn her that the men were approaching, but all was quiet. She did not know how long she had been in the cave. It had been dark for such a long time, and even if the sun had risen outside, in here the world was black. Rihani looked into the darkness around her and felt confused. "Which way did I come? I will never be able to find my way out. If I go the wrong way I will be lost forever underneath the mountain," she thought. "I need to find the power again. The power will give me the strength and courage to find my way outside again," she continued more confidently.

She performed the same ritual as before and again could feel herself become stronger. She lightly ran her hands over the sides of the cave and felt the rugged edges of the limestone wall. "If only I could cut these ropes, my hands could be free and then I could untie the ropes on my feet, and I could walk," she reasoned. After a few attempts of feeling across the dark floor of the cave for a sharp stone, she found one and started scraping the rope that bound her against it. The pain was excruciating, for the more pressure she put onto the ropes, the more they cut into her wet, slippery skin.

At first nothing happened and she felt her efforts would prove futile. But she would not give way to her despair and kept rubbing the ropes until finally she felt them loosen and was able to release her hands. Her feet were much easier to untie. Once freed, she could start to feel the blood circulating again throughout her sore, bruised and bloodied limbs. Rihani tried to stand up, but fell to her knees. She tried again and again without success. Her head became dizzy and her legs trembled. She withdrew into herself and again gathered the mana that surrounded her as she called upon the spirits of her ancestors. "Ekewane, help me" she cried.

When she felt the strength enter her, she tried again to stand. Her first attempts were again in vain, but then finally she was able to stand up, holding onto the sides of the cave. Rihani was still fearful and uncertain. "What should I do now? Should I keep hiding for a while longer or go back to the entrance of the cave? Will the men have gone? I am so tired and thirsty. If I stay here I will surely die anyway. I will go back, but first I must find a large, sharp rock to defend myself with if the men are still there," she continued, whispering into the cave. She started feeling around again on the floor of the cave.

The rocks her hands encountered were solid and large, and she could not pry any loose, so she kept digging around on her hands and knees. At one point, she became aware of something sharp. It felt like a large shell so she picked it up. It was fairly large and was connected to other, smaller shells by a string. Around the edges of the larger shell, she could feel there were small shells. They were woven onto it as if in decoration. Unbeknownst to her, it was a shell armband. Rihani did not know this, nor how it ended up buried deep in this cave, but she understood that her discovery was important. "Is this what I was asked to find?" she thought to herself.

"Which way is the entrance?" she asked next. Then, as she looked around, she saw a faint, hazy light in the distance. "Maybe it is the entrance? But I have travelled a long way from there. It could be another entrance, or maybe it is a spirit that lives in this cave. Or it could be the torch of the men who have come looking for me." Rihani, unsure of what to do, started trembling. But yet again she remembered Ekewane and how she was willing to risk her own life for her people. "She must have been afraid to stand up in front of the warring tribes. I can be brave too, for she is my ancestor."

Slowly and determinedly, she started making her way

towards the faint light, hoping that she was going in the right direction and that the light did not belong to something evil. She walked slowly and unsteadily, always holding onto to the side of the tunnel. Every now and again she would stop and listen, but apart from her own breathing, everything was quiet. Rihani finally saw the entrance of the cave and stumbled towards it. She was exhausted, but needed desperately to return to her family. So, with all the strength remaining to her, she started hurrying down the steep slope. She kept slipping and sliding. Every now and again she would trip over a rock or a root of a tree and fall heavily to the ground with the air often knocked out of her lungs. She would then have to wait a few moments to catch her breath before painfully standing up to walk again.

Over and over she fell, but kept holding tightly onto the precious armband. At one stage she stopped, confused, "Am I going the right direction?" she asked aloud. Rihani looked, stunned, at the now familiar faint haze further down the track in front of her and felt her body grow cold. Was this the spirit of an ancestor? "Ekewane?" she called out, but the faint haze only shifted further away. She felt exhausted and so thirsty, but forced herself to follow the light. It had helped her out of the cave and it would help her find her way home, she thought. Rihani looked up through the trees at the moon. It shone so brightly that in places she thought it might be the sun. She was exhausted but kept walking, clutching the precious armband and chanting softly to herself, invoking to her ancestors to help her reach her home.

Chapter Fourteen
Retaliation

Aio, Gadiya, Itu and Avery, together with other men from the tribes living on the island, lay close to the ground. Akau was also there. He had come with his father, who was the chief of the Yarle clan. He was frantic with worry about Rihani. The men waited quietly for the beachcombers to return to their camp. Aio knew that the intruders had powerful weapons, so he decided they would wait and attack them whilst they slept. The sun was slowly sinking over the horizon as the men lay in the shadows of the undergrowth surrounding the beachcombers' camp. The only sound came from the wind whistling through the trees and the waves that gently crashed onto the shore. An angry, ear-piecing scream from the mountain tore into the silence. "Eigara has sent the spirits from the mountain!" whispered Aio.

Avery felt his heart pounding. His breathing was fast and shallow. He felt the thrum of his blood running through his veins and around him the noises of the night were magnified. He had killed before but he still felt nauseated when he remembered it. Now he was frightened he could not do it again. "Rihani," he whispered.

The image of Eigara's face during the last ritual he witnessed flashed across his mind. It had been so full of hate and black magic that she no longer resembled the same woman. He had always felt that she had a strong inner power and now he had seen some of that power. "This island has many dark secrets. Could Rihani also perform this black magic if she wanted to destroy her enemies?" he thought. If Rihani were dead, he would lose all his faith in caring for someone. She was his first and his best friend, but he realised she was more than that too. He did not want to think about this. His feelings were unfamiliar and he was too afraid to try to understand them. He had always accepted the abuse given to him over the years, but things were different with Rihani. Beautiful, happy Rihani. He felt his hands grip his spear with such force that his fingers grew numb. He imagined what the three men could do to her. She was defenceless against their brutal strength. Avery had seen in the dark alleys of London the violence a man could do to women, and he shuddered at the memory. At the time, he had kept his head down and walked away as fast as he could. Now, he could see Rihani lying bloodied and violated. He felt a surge of blood to his head, and for the first time in his life, he hated with a fierce intensity. "Eigara's magic is real. These men have brought the ugliness of my past to this island," he thought. The high-pitched scream come again from the mountain and echoed throughout the shoreline, reinforcing Avery's conviction.

Owen, Briggs and Liam finally staggered, intoxicated, back into their camp. They had been drinking all day. The girl they captured had disappeared. They had looked for her for a little while, but it seemed she had just vanished. They reasoned they could very easily capture another young girl, and so returned to their encampment. They built up the fire and sat around drinking from the containers they carried with them. They then cooked some meat and ate it, drinking all the while, and laughing.

Aio could not see Rihani anywhere and silently called upon his ancestors with the hope that she was still alive somewhere on the island.

Despite his drunkenness, Liam felt uneasy. The hair at the back of his neck bristled and he gazed around suspiciously. In London, he had often felt like this. It was a sense of imminent danger, but he dismissed the feeling, believing it to be caused by the incessant and unnerving howling from the mountain. "We are the most powerful people on this island. These natives are only savages and we have the guns," he reassured himself.

Well into the night, the beachcombers finally fell asleep. Aio was surprised that they did not keep watch. "They are so sure of themselves. They are unaware that they have committed many taboos and now the spirits demand their lives," he whispered to his men. Eigara had already called to the spirit world, so he knew that the strangers were already lost. He and his men would only have to complete the deed. Finally, Aio gave the signal to attack. The beachcombers jumped up, startled and ready to fire their guns. They staggered a little as they were still intoxicated. They commenced firing indiscriminately.

Owen hit one of the men who fell to the ground. He did not have time to pick up his second gun as a large native was upon him, so he plunged his bayonet at him. But before he could reach the man, he heard a loud blast and felt a dull pain in his chest. He thought that Briggs or Liam had misfired. "Why did they shoot me?" he thought as he dropped to the ground. Briggs had discharged both of his guns and was now having a hand-to-hand fight with a native. He had the upper hand, as his bayonet kept the

Islander at bay, but then felt a sharp pain to his head and he lost consciousness. Liam felt a strange, sharp pain to his stomach and looked down, confused to find a spear embedded in his stomach. He looked around to see if he could see Briggs and Owen, but all he could see was a mass of angry natives who were screaming. Dazed, he felt his knees give way and he fell to the ground.

The intruders were all dead, but some of the Islanders had also been killed or wounded. Aio ordered the men to build stretches. The men rolled the bodies of the pale men onto them. They did not touch the dead bodies of these men, because they were taboo. If they did touch them, they themselves would become contaminated. The dead and wounded men of the clans were carried back to their villages where their sorcerers could help heal or bury them. Aio ordered that the dead beachcombers be thrown into a deep pit on the side of the mountain. To bury them would offend their gods.

Eigara stood in front of the altar, chanting. The people of the village sat in silence and only Eigara's chant could be heard above the sounds of the waves as they hit the shoreline. Then she turned and whispered, "Our gods and the spirits of our ancestors are angry. These men who have come from afar came from a place of great evil, and this powerful dark spirit has brought great suffering to our land. Our spirits are also angry because we have spilt blood on our island." As Eigara spoke, she looked into the distance. A young girl was slowly staggering towards her. Her heart leapt "RIHANI!" she cried out.

The people turned to look where Eigara was pointing. They all rose together and ran towards Rihani.

"Mother," Rihani whispered as she collapsed to the ground, still grasping her shell armband. Rihani was taken to her hut and laid on her mat. Her mother and the other women of the village slowly cleansed her wet, soiled and bloodied body. She was covered in blood from the scratches and cuts from the sharp rocks and branches. Rihani could feel the cool water sting her flesh, but she did not move. She could not. Her body was spent.

When the women had finish cleaning her, Eigara lifted her daughter's head and gently held a shell filled with fresh water to her lips. Rihani felt the cool water and opened her lips and let the drops trickle down her parched, swollen throat. Then she heard her mother whisper, "Sleep, Rihani. Our ancestors will guard you."
The night was long. The people of the island were too afraid to sleep and huddled around the fires at the centre of each village. A taboo had been broken, blood had been spilt on their island, and the gods would be very angry.

The next morning, when Rihani opened her eyes, the bright sun was filtering through the thatched walls of her hut. Ema and her cousins were still sleeping. "Maybe it was all a dream?" she thought. But as she tried to stand up, she felt dizzy and nauseous. Pain rippled through her body and she had to lie back down. She waited until Ema woke up. Her sister smiled at her. "We were so worried about you. Where have you been?"

Rihani nodded her head and asked for water, which Eigara had left in a coconut shell beside her mat. As she was drinking, her mother and father came to the entrance of the hut.

"The pale skinned men! They will kill us!" Rihani

exclaimed, terrified. She was still confused about the events that happened.

"They have gone to the spirit world," stated Aio proudly.

Eigara looked sadly at her daughter. She knew that the gods would now punish the Islanders for these killings.

"What happened to you?" Aio asked.

"I was hit over the head and taken to a cave. Deep inside the cave, I found the shells tied together with a string. When I went back to the entrance of the cave, the three men had left. I was so afraid but kept walking. I saw a light when I thought I was lost and followed it home. What do those shells I found mean?" Rihani asked her parents.

"It is the armband that is mentioned in our legends. It belonged to our powerful chief, Erangue. It is a sign of great power and respect and was given only to one man in a village. It was lost and it is said that it will only return when our people are in danger and are greatly in need of help from our ancestors," Eigara explained.

Aio took the armband and placed it around his neck. Ordinarily it would be worn around his arm, but he was afraid that he would lose it whilst in combat. He knew that the other clans would respect his power even more now that he had the shell armband. The people of the island had heard about the legendary armband, but had never seen one. Rihani was his daughter and the spirits of their ancestors had helped her find the armband for him, the Head Chief.

Rihani's experience in the cave made her stronger. She knew that the people on their island would now look at her differently, more like they did her mother. "I am a sorceress! My ancestors' magic blood runs in my veins. I will never let another person frighten or hurt me again," she promised herself.

Chapter Fifteen
Dark Legacy

The island was shrouded in heavy, dark rain clouds. The rain continued pouring down on the villages as people tried to bury their dead. The spirits of the dead were joining their ancestors, for if an Islander died and it rained, their spirits were deemed as having lived an honourable life. The tribes around the island carried out the death rituals of their ancestors. There were feasts in honour of the dead. It was the way of the people to mourn their departed loved ones. The bodies were then buried near their family homes with some of their prized possessions. The spirits of these possessions would accompany the dead warrior. Some of the men were buried out at sea, according to the wishes of the families.

When the ceremonies were concluded, the people living on the island tried to return to the tranquillity of their lives before the arrival of the beachcombers. However, their serenity did not last very long. A dark spirit had entered into the bodies of many of the people. The Islanders had never seen this strange illness before, so they knew that an evil spirit was amongst them. Even their sorcerers did not know how to help the sick.

The first signs that something was very wrong started with the small children. The first two years of a child's life had always been a dangerous time and when the child turned two, there had always been a great celebration. Many children died during their first two years, so at first people ignored the strange symptoms. The small children would develop a high fever, they would lay listlessly in the arms of their mothers or other members of the family for many days, and then they died.

Before long, however, many adults also started feeling unwell. They felt tired and had headaches. Then a high fever set in and red spots appeared on their tongues and in their mouths, after which a rash spread all over their bodies starting on their faces. The rash soon turned into raised bumps which would fill with a thick, opaque pus. Blisters would also cover the victims' tongues and the inside of their mouths. Their faces and bodies became covered with sores oozing this thick pus. The people on the island once again were terrified. They did not have time to bury their dead, but those still strong enough would build platforms and carry the bodies up unto the mountain and drop them into the deep crevices.

"The pale men have brought this evil spirit to our island. Now we will all die," the natives would cry.

Those who had not been taken by this mysterious illness tried to help their family members who were sick. Eigara, Rihani and Ema collected ingredients to make the poultices they had always used for infections, but these were of little help. Often the three women would sit in Eigara's hut and invoke their gods and ancestors, but the power of the dark spirit brought to the island by the pale men was very strong and people kept dying. All around the island, the villagers made sacrifices, and gifts of food and water were placed on the stone altars in every village. But still their people died. The incessant rain kept pouring down as the Islanders scurried around their villagers.

Rihani helped her mother make the poultices and pray to their gods and ancestors, but she remained despondent. She had seen this happen and knew that many more of their people would become ill and die. The gods had decreed it, as it was to be their punishment for breaking a taboo. Avery tried to go about his daily routine, attempting to ignore the burning in his throat. He felt very hot and even the rain constantly battering him did not cool him down. He felt weak and his legs trembled as he tried to walk back to his hut and lie down. He barely managed to reach his hut before he collapsed and the world around him went black. Aio and his family were horrified by this, as none of the people who became sick had survived, and so the spirits would take him too. Again, Avery's life was in danger.

"I do not know why the spirits keep wanting to take this boy into their world," Eigara uttered sadly to her husband.

"Our ancestors are strong and they have saved him before. We will pray to them again for help. This boy is now part of our family and he belongs to us," confirmed Aio to his wife.

Eiaraga wanted to help Avery herself. She thought that if another woman were to touch him, the evil spirit within him would also enter her. But Rihani insisted that she would help Avery. She felt strong and was now a sorceress. Her mother had many other sick people to attend to, so Eigara permitted Rihani to stay with Avery and help him.

"Rihani, if you remain with Avery you will have to follow strict instructions. It is taboo for you to eat fish or meat. You may only eat a small amount of yams in the morning. You must not drink coconut water or milk. You are only to drink the water from the ponds once a day. We will bring you food and drink, for you must not leave the hut during the day," Eigara warned her daughter.

Rihani knelt beside the mat that Avery had been laid upon. He had been isolated from the hut where he normally slept. She looked at him and could feel his spirit slowly leaving him. She felt a deep, empty hole within herself. As she watched Avery struggle to breathe, she felt this hole increasing in size until the darkness she felt within shrouded her. Desperate, she started to chant. The chant was not one that her mother had taught her, but came from deep within. She held her hands above his body and slowly withdrew into herself.

She felt as if she had entered into him, into part of Avery himself. There was darkness inside. Only a faint light flicked within and she followed it. She found herself inside his heart. It was pumping and with each whooshing sound, like the waves crashing against the reef, the blood would rush past her. But the rhythm was weakening. Instinctively, she put out her hands and touched the organ. It was warm and soft. She closed her eyes and put as much of her own light as she could onto Avery's feeble heart.

Her body suddenly jerked awake. Stunned, she looked around. She felt her hands tingle and looked at them, confused. "Had it been a dream?" Rihani asked herself. She felt exhausted, drained. She looked down at Avery's listless body and the tears trickled down her face. She felt so tired, but she would not give up fighting for Avery's life.

Rihani constantly bathed Avery with water from the sacred pool. The women of her village took it in turns to keep the constant supply of water. She would then cover his body in a sticky poultice and invoked the help of her ancestors, especially Ekewane. She did not sleep, for she knew that if she did, his spirit would leave him. Her tiredness left her dazed and confused. Her ministrations had become instinctive. Days had become nights and then days again. Time had no meaning as she sat by his side.

Rihani felt as if she was tied by an invisible thread to his heart. She could see a faint glow surrounding his body. The light was his life force. She needed to keep vigilant so it would not die out. She chanted, invoking help from her ancestors, until she could no longer feel her own body. She could only feel the thread that tied him to her. Sadness overwhelmed her and old doubts and anxieties slowly pervaded her mind. "I have seen into the future. But the sight did not bring me happiness. It brought me pain and hopelessness, for I can do nothing to stop it from happening. I cannot help Avery. Soon people will come to me for help, but I also have the power to harm. I saw my mother's beautiful face change with the power of evil. Will I too have this power? I am afraid of this dark power. I do not know if I could control it. Is my power a gift or a curse? I cannot save my family. I cannot save my people. I cannot save Avery."

Rihanii felt a weight beyond time. It was of all her past ancestors. She felt the heaviness of the expectations of her people. Would she have the power to heal or only to kill? She trembled at the thought of this dark power. "Will I be able to carry this burden? I am a sorceress! I will help my people," she whispered aloud.

The days followed the same routine. Every morning, Eigara and Ema brought food, water and poultices to the hut. One morning Rihani asked her mother, "In my dream I saw our people dying of this evil spirit that is eating our flesh. Can we do no more to help?"

Eigara looked sadly at her daughter. "We can only pray to our gods and ancestors. The evil spirit these pale men have brought is strong, but our gods and ancestors are stronger. I have left offerings at the altar of our gods. I have also sacrificed some of our animals. People are dying all over the island. It is a grave time, but we must keep praying to our gods and ancestors, for only they have the power to help us."

Avery felt as if he were burning up. He felt exhausted. His life had been so difficult. Only now, on this island, did he at last feel safe and free, but he no longer had the strength to live. He prayed to any god who would listen to help him leave this earth and the body that had pained him so much.

Rihani continued to invoke their gods and Ekewane to help him, but he was getting worse. The rasping sound of Avery's laboured breath told her that his spirit would soon leave his body. Tears of desperation flowed down her face. She was looking at him when the light she had seen encasing him appeared to swirl up and leave his body. She lowered her head and fell into a deep trance. Once again she saw herself leaving her body. She stood up, looking at both herself and Avery. She watched again as the hazy light that flowed from Avery's body materialised into a phantasmagorical image of him. He looked at her, no longer in pain and smiled.

"I must go now," he said.

"NO! NO! It is not your time to leave for the spirit world," she cried.

"I am so tired. I have been happy on this island, but now it is time for me to go. You must cut the thread that binds me to you and let me go," Avery said sadly.

"No, it is not your time! Because . . . if you go now, you take our unborn children with you. You must come back to me. You must fight the spirits that are taking you!" cried Rihani. She did not know how those thoughts had entered her mind. Rihani then started chanting a strange prayer. She became aware of her body swaying from side to side as she sang the powerful sacred prayer.

For many more days Avery lay unconscious. His body was still hot and burning. No matter how many times her mother tried to convince her, Rihani would not leave his side. The spirits of the mountain screamed continuously, as if they too felt the pain of the people on the island. The rain kept pouring down. The weeks past slowly as more and more people kept dying. Then, just as everyone lost hope and thought that they would all perish, their gods started taking pity on them. Some of the infected people had survived, but their faces and bodies were left scarred and they would never have beautiful, smooth skin that was free of blemishes again.

Avery's fever broke early one morning. He was one of the fortunate ones. The spirits had spared his life once again. He was aware that Rihani had nursed him back from death. He remembered a strange dream he had whilst he was still very sick. This was curious because otherwise he could only remember the feeling of his body being on fire and the excruciating pain he felt all over, especially when he tried to breath. He remembered a strange sensation, as if he was floating. Then, looking down on his body, he had thought that he had died, but Rihani was also there in his dream. She was crying and kept persuading him to return to his body. At first he had refused, but then she had said the strangest thing: that if he died, their children would also die with him. Avery felt confused, as he had never really thought of Rihani as being a future wife for him.

Rihani had changed since her experience with the beachcombers. There was something deep and mystic about her, like her mother Eigara. At times, Avery felt uncomfortable and almost afraid of her. Th ere were things on this island he could not explain and Rihani was part of these mysteries. Here, on the island the people were not governed by money, but by ancient traditions and superstitions. These were things he knew little about. His life before the island had been painful, but it contained many marvels that the people on the island could never even imagine. At the time, he had been too poor to appreciate these marvels. But still, the fancy coaches and beautiful houses, the roads and tall majestic buildings and bridges had all existed in his world and he sometimes missed them. Rihani was his friend Gadiya's sister and the daughter of Eigara and Aio. To marry her would be impossible for him, as she would eventually marry a son of one of the powerful chiefs on the island. Most probably, it would be Akau "Where do I belong?" sighed Avery.

Rihani also remembered the experience she had whilst nursing Avery. She too had never thought about being married to Avery before, but the dream was very real, and she now knew she could see into the future.

At first, she felt embarrassed when she met Avery as he recovered from his illness, although was not very often, as he also seemed to want to avoid her. Rihani finally reasoned that Avery was too sick at the time and would not remember that strange encounter. But now she was tormented by different thoughts.

"Avery is different. He has accepted our world, but does not really understand the fundamental beliefs of our culture that were founded before time. Will he ever truly believe and be one of our people? I cannot marry him. I am a sorceress with powerful magical powers. My family and my people will depend on me. One day I will take my mother's place. Ewekane once loved someone from the Sitio tribe. Avery is from a different world. I cannot marry him. I must marry someone from our island. Perhaps it will be Akau, but I only saw Avery in my future!" she sighed, confused.

Chapter Sixteen
Missionaries

Mother Hubbard Dress

The island was shrouded in heavy, dark rain clouds. The

rain continued pouring down on the villages as people tried to bury their dead. The spirits of the dead were joining their ancestors, for if an Islander died and it rained, their spirits were deemed as having lived an honourable life. The tribes around the island carried out the death rituals of their ancestors. There were feasts in honour of the dead. It was the way of the people to mourn their departed loved ones. The bodies were then buried near their family homes with some of their prized possessions. The spirits of these possessions would accompany the dead warrior. Some of the men were buried out at sea, according to the wishes of the families.

When the ceremonies were concluded, the people living on the island tried to return to the tranquillity of their lives before the arrival of the beachcombers. However, their serenity did not last very long. A dark spirit had entered into the bodies of many of the people. The Islanders had never seen this strange illness before, so they knew that an evil spirit was amongst them. Even their sorcerers did not know how to help the sick.

The first signs that something was very wrong started with the small children. The first two years of a child's life had always been a dangerous time and when the child turned two, there had always been a great celebration. Many children died during their first two years, so at first people ignored the strange symptoms. The small children would develop a high fever, they would lay listlessly in the arms of their mothers or other members of the family for many days, and then they died.

Before long, however, many adults also started feeling unwell. They felt tired and had headaches. Then a high fever set in and red spots appeared on their tongues and in their mouths, after which a rash spread all over their bodies starting on their faces. The rash soon turned into raised bumps which would fill with a thick, opaque pus. Blisters would also cover the victims' tongues and the inside of their mouths. Their faces and bodies became covered with sores oozing this thick pus. The people on the island once again were terrified. They did not have time to bury their dead, but those still strong enough would build platforms and carry the bodies up unto the mountain and drop them into the deep crevices.

"The pale men have brought this evil spirit to our island. Now we will all die," the natives would cry.

Those who had not been taken by this mysterious illness tried to help their family members who were sick. Eigara, Rihani and Ema collected ingredients to make the poultices they had always used for infections, but these were of little help. Often the three women would sit in Eigara's hut and invoke their gods and ancestors, but the power of the dark spirit brought to the island by the pale men was very strong and people kept dying. All around the island, the villagers made sacrifices, and gifts of food and water were placed on the stone altars in every village. But still their people died. The incessant rain kept pouring down as the Islanders scurried around their villagers.

Rihani helped her mother make the poultices and pray to their gods and ancestors, but she remained despondent. She had seen this happen and knew that many more of their people would become ill and die. The gods had decreed it, as it was to be their punishment for breaking a taboo. Avery tried to go about his daily routine, attempting to ignore the burning in his throat. He felt very hot and even the rain constantly battering him did not cool him down. He felt weak and his legs trembled as he tried to walk back to his hut and lie down. He barely managed to reach his hut before he collapsed and the world around him went black. Aio and his family were horrified by this, as none of the people who became sick had survived, and so the spirits would take him too. Again, Avery's life was in danger.

"I do not know why the spirits keep wanting to take this boy into their world," Eigara uttered sadly to her husband.

"Our ancestors are strong and they have saved him before. We will pray to them again for help. This boy is now part of our family and he belongs to us," confirmed Aio to his wife.

Eiaraga wanted to help Avery herself. She thought that if another woman were to touch him, the evil spirit within him would also enter her. But Rihani insisted that she would help Avery. She felt strong and was now a sorceress. Her mother had many other sick people to attend to, so Eigara permitted Rihani to stay with Avery and help him.

"Rihani, if you remain with Avery you will have to follow strict instructions. It is taboo for you to eat fish or meat. You may only eat a small amount of yams in the morning. You must not drink coconut water or milk. You are only to drink the water from the ponds once a day. We will bring you food and drink, for you must not leave the hut during the day," Eigara warned her daughter.

Rihani knelt beside the mat that Avery had been laid upon. He had been isolated from the hut where he normally slept. She looked at him and could feel his spirit slowly leaving him. She felt a deep, empty hole within herself. As she watched Avery struggle to breathe, she felt this hole increasing in size until the darkness she felt within shrouded her. Desperate, she started to chant. The chant was not one that her mother had taught her, but came from deep within. She held her hands above his body and slowly withdrew into herself.

She felt as if she had entered into him, into part of Avery himself. There was darkness inside. Only a faint light flicked within and she followed it. She found herself inside his heart. It was pumping and with each whooshing sound, like the waves crashing against the reef, the blood would rush past her. But the rhythm was weakening. Instinctively, she put out her hands and touched the organ. It was warm and soft. She closed her eyes and put as much of her own light as she could onto Avery's feeble heart.

Her body suddenly jerked awake. Stunned, she looked around. She felt her hands tingle and looked at them, confused. "Had it been a dream?" Rihani asked herself. She felt exhausted, drained. She looked down at Avery's listless body and the tears trickled down her face. She felt so tired, but she would not give up fighting for Avery's life. Rihani constantly bathed Avery with water from the sacred pool. The women of her village took it in turns to keep the constant supply of water. She would then cover his body in a sticky poultice and invoked the help of her ancestors, especially Ekewane. She did not sleep, for she knew that if she did, his spirit would leave him. Her tiredness left her dazed and confused. Her ministrations had become instinctive. Days had become nights and then days again. Time had no meaning as she sat by his side.

Rihani felt as if she was tied by an invisible thread to his heart. She could see a faint glow surrounding his body. The light was his life force. She needed to keep vigilant so it would not die out. She chanted, invoking help from her ancestors, until she could no longer feel her own body. She could only feel the thread that tied him to her. Sadness overwhelmed her and old doubts and anxieties slowly pervaded her mind. "I have seen into the future. But the sight did not bring me happiness. It brought me pain and hopelessness, for I can do nothing to stop it from happening. I cannot help Avery. Soon people will come to me for help, but I also have the power to harm. I saw my mother's beautiful face change with the power of evil. Will I too have this power? I am afraid of this dark power. I do not know if I could control it. Is my power a gift or a curse? I cannot save my family. I cannot save my people. I cannot save Avery."

Rihanii felt a weight beyond time. It was of all her past ancestors. She felt the heaviness of the expectations of her people. Would she have the power to heal or only to kill? She trembled at the thought of this dark power. "Will I be able to carry this burden? I am a sorceress! I will help my people," she whispered aloud.

The days followed the same routine. Every morning, Eigara and Ema brought food, water and poultices to the hut. One morning Rihani asked her mother, "In my dream I saw our people dying of this evil spirit that is eating our flesh. Can we do no more to help?"

Eigara looked sadly at her daughter. "We can only pray to our gods and ancestors. The evil spirit these pale men have brought is strong, but our gods and ancestors are stronger. I have left offerings at the altar of our gods. I have also sacrificed some of our animals. People are dying all over the island. It is a grave time, but we must keep praying to our gods and ancestors, for only they have the power to help us."

Avery felt as if he were burning up. He felt exhausted. His life had been so difficult. Only now, on this island, did he at last feel safe and free, but he no longer had the strength to live. He prayed to any god who would listen to help him leave this earth and the body that had pained him so much.

Rihani continued to invoke their gods and Ekewane to help him, but he was getting worse. The rasping sound of Avery's laboured breath told her that his spirit would soon leave his body. Tears of desperation flowed down her face. She was looking at him when the light she had seen encasing him appeared to swirl up and leave his body. She lowered her head and fell into a deep trance. Once again she saw herself leaving her body. She stood up, looking at both herself and Avery. She watched again as the hazy light that flowed from Avery's body materialised into a phantasmagorical image of him. He looked at her, no longer in pain and smiled.

"I must go now," he said.

"NO! NO! It is not your time to leave for the spirit world," she cried.

"I am so tired. I have been happy on this island, but now it is time for me to go. You must cut the thread that binds me to you and let me go," Avery said sadly.

"No, it is not your time! Because . . . if you go now, you

take our unborn children with you. You must come back to me. You must fight the spirits that are taking you!" cried Rihani. She did not know how those thoughts had entered her mind. Rihani then started chanting a strange prayer. She became aware of her body swaying from side to side as she sang the powerful sacred prayer.

For many more days Avery lay unconscious. His body was still hot and burning. No matter how many times her mother tried to convince her, Rihani would not leave his side. The spirits of the mountain screamed continuously, as if they too felt the pain of the people on the island. The rain kept pouring down. The weeks past slowly as more and more people kept dying. Then, just as everyone lost hope and thought that they would all perish, their gods started taking pity on them. Some of the infected people had survived, but their faces and bodies were left scarred and they would never have beautiful, smooth skin that was free of blemishes again.

Avery's fever broke early one morning. He was one of the fortunate ones. The spirits had spared his life once again. He was aware that Rihani had nursed him back from death. He remembered a strange dream he had whilst he was still very sick. This was curious because otherwise he could only remember the feeling of his body being on fire and the excruciating pain he felt all over, especially when he tried to breath. He remembered a strange sensation, as if he was floating. Then, looking down on his body, he had thought that he had died, but Rihani was also there in his dream. She was crying and kept persuading him to return to his body. At first he had refused, but then she had said the strangest thing: that if he died, their children would also die with him. Avery felt confused, as he had never really thought of Rihani as being a future wife for him.

Rihani had changed since her experience with the beachcombers. There was something deep and mystic about her, like her mother Eigara. At times, Avery felt uncomfortable and almost afraid of her. Th ere were things on this island he could not explain and Rihani was part of these mysteries. Here, on the island the people were not governed by money, but by ancient traditions and superstitions. These were things he knew little about. His life before the island had been painful, but it contained many marvels that the people on the island could never even imagine. At the time, he had been too poor to appreciate these marvels. But still, the fancy coaches and beautiful houses, the roads and tall majestic buildings and bridges had all existed in his world and he sometimes missed them. Rihani was his friend Gadiya's sister and the daughter of Eigara and Aio. To marry her would be impossible for him, as she would eventually marry a son of one of the powerful chiefs on the island. Most probably, it would be Akau "Where do I belong?" sighed Avery.

Rihani also remembered the experience she had whilst nursing Avery. She too had never thought about being married to Avery before, but the dream was very real, and she now knew she could see into the future. At first, she felt embarrassed when she met Avery as he recovered from his illness, although was not very often, as he also seemed to want to avoid her. Rihani finally reasoned that Avery was too sick at the time and would not remember that strange encounter. But now she was tormented by different thoughts.

"Avery is different. He has accepted our world, but does not really understand the fundamental beliefs of our culture that were founded before time. Will he ever truly believe and be one of our people? I cannot marry him. I am a sorceress with powerful magical powers. My family and my people will depend on me. One day I will take my mother's place. Ewekane once loved someone from the Sitio tribe. Avery is from a different world. I cannot marry him. I must marry someone from our island. Perhaps it will be Akau, but I only saw Avery in my future!" she sighed, confused.

Chapter Seventeen
Nasi

Nasi noticed the two missionaries were always watching him. He was suspicious of them. "What if their god is greater than my gods and the spirits of my ancestors?" he often questioned himself since the arrival of the two missionaries. Nasi belonged to the Iwa clan. He was an only child, for his siblings had all died. Like all the children on the island, he had been pampered by the adults. During his childhood, he played and joined in with the other children of the village. It was when he reached puberty that things began to change and he started feeling different. He was not interested in flirting with the girls and nor did he desire them. He preferred to be alone, just watching other boys at their activities.

Nasi had always known that he would not marry. The very idea of it disgusted him. He kept these thoughts to himself because he knew no one would understand. He liked some of the boys in the village, and Aio in particular. Aio was always friendly to him and often asked him to join in with whatever activity he was doing. Aio, even as a young boy, stood out. He was taller and more muscular than the other boys of his age. He could fish, swim and dance better than the others. Nasi had always admired him and wished he had been born more like him. Then Aio married Eigara and left the village; this left Nasi feeling lonely, angry and betrayed. However, it was also at this time that his life began to change. The old sorcerer of the village who did not have any children to pass his magical knowledge down to had picked him to become his apprentice. Nasi's parents were thrilled and for a time he concentrated on his apprenticeship.

He had not inherited his magic, so his learning had been long and difficult. His apprenticeship had been hard for him and he especially hated all the taboos that went with his long training. Often he had gone without food for many days. After years of preparation, his initiation had finally come. His final initiation ceremony had been painful and his body still bore the scars of it. Not long after the old sorcerer died, Nasi finally became the sorcerer of his village. It was a position of power and respect. However, like many of the other sorcerers on the island, he was very jealous of Eigara, for the power and respect shown to her outweighed all of them. The people of the island went to her when their own sorcerer could not help them. Eigara had also stolen Aio from Nasi's village and he always felt a searing hatred towards her.

Eigara was born into a powerful family of sorceresses, while Nasi had only been chosen by his old village sorcerer and had to be trained for many years. Nasi knew that there were two types of magic: the good and the dark. He had persuaded the old sorcerer to teach him both types. The old sorcerer had done so, but warned him that black magic was very risky.

"Magic is very powerful. For every curse there is a price. And if the spells and chants are not accurately performed, you will risk your own life," the old master would often say.

Nasi dreamed of the day he would destroy Eigara. He would prove to Aio and all others that he was the greatest, the most powerful sorcerer on the islander. However, Eigara's ancestors were very potent and he was too afraid to cast a black spell on her. So he waited and fervently practiced his magic.

One day as the two missionaries watched him, he approached and sat down beside them. Joseph and Patrick knew that this was their chance. The sorcerer was interested in their god. So began the conversion of Nasi to the new religion. Nasi listened to the two men talk in his own language about their powerful god. He was told that their god was the creator of all. He listened when they told him about the miracles he had performed. He had brought people back from the spirit world, he had walked on the sea, he had made food for many when there was little, and he cured people when they were dying or could not walk. Nasi became convinced that if he prayed to their new god, as well as his old gods, he would become the most powerful sorcerer the people of the island had ever known. He would be even greater than Ekewane!

Joseph and Patrick were delighted to know that Nasi would speak to the Islanders and have them take part in their services. The two men dreamed of the many wonderful gifts of food and other valuable items they would receive from their congregation. They would eventually have power over the people of the island. They reasoned that once the Islanders were converted, God would punish them if they did not continue to participate in the mission and bring gifts in thanks. Nasi started attending the rituals the two missionaries often performed. He was captivated as they prayed and ate the bread they said was the body of their god and they drank his blood. Nasi had never tasted a human body before and felt elated by this act. Even if it was not a real body, he could feel the power of it grow within him. The two missionaries told him again their stories of the miracles performed by their god. This new god could bring people back from the spirit world. Nasi knew that Eiagara could not do this. This god also made two fish become many so that many people could be fed. The more the missionaries spoke of their god, the more Nasi was convinced that he too could make these miracles happen.

Nasi persuaded some of the other Islanders to attend the missionaries' teachings and rituals. The Islanders who attend these rituals did not truly understand their meaning, but they enjoyed the elaborate ceremonies. The missionaries had brought with them a fine, brightly woven fabric they called 'cloth', and convinced the women to cover their bodies with this, as they said being dressed in only a grass skirt was a 'sin' and against the teachings of their god. The women did not understand this but they liked the feel and colour of the cloth. They learnt how to make what the missionaries called 'Mother Hubbard' dresses. These dresses they wore on top of their grass skirts, but this made the women hot and many complained. The missionaries explained that to get to the spirit world, they had to suffer, and so they women kept wearing the 'Mother Hubbard' dresses.

The people who converted to Christianity were forbidden to dance, for they were told dancing too would anger this new god. But they did not want to stop their dancing and singing, as these had been an important part of their tradition and their lives. Some of the Islanders found secret places where, late at night, they would gather and dance. Patrick and Joseph also convinced the families who attended their services to destroy their altars. "God will become angry if you pray to your old gods and spirits!" they said. The missionaries also demanded more offerings as payment to their god.

Nasi stood beside his limestone altar that was hidden deep in the forest, away from all the villages. It took him a long time to reach this altar, but he needed to be alone to work his magic. The clearing had a natural limestone table cut into the pinnacle and this was what Nasi used as his altar. Around the clearing he hung various crosses of all sizes, which he made by tying two sticks together in the middle. The altar had a larger cross in the same size as the one the missionaries had on their altar. Beside his forest altar, Nasi kept variously sized woven caskets, coconut and shell containers. In these he kept secret objects used for his spells. He was convinced that if he harnessed the power of this new god he could destroy his enemies, especially Eigara.

He had brought with him a chicken hidden in a casket as he made his way through the undergrowth and he was perspiring from the humidity, for there was no breeze beneath the thick undergrowth. When he finally reached his alcove, he sat down and took a long drink from a coconut shell filled with toddy. He waited for a long time, for he had to gather his strength and needed the inebriated feeling of the alcoholic drink to make feel his body light and dispel all worldly thoughts from his mind. Only then could he call upon the gods and spirits. When he finally felt ready, he stood up. He started chanting over and over again, "Wai-Iu-Eig-Wai. Wai-Iu-Eig-Wai. Wai-Iu-

Eig-Wai."
With the toddy in full affect, Nasi felt it was now the right time, so he took the chicken from the casket, still chanting all the while. At this stage, his body felt invaded by a stronger force. He slowly laid the chicken on his altar and plunged a sharp, tapered stone, into its heart. The chicken quivered for a few moments then lay still. Nasi then pulled out a large shell and let the blood of the chicken trickle into it. When he had enough blood, he lifted the shell into the air as he had seen the missionaries do. Still chanting, he lowered the shell and drank the blood. His chanting was becoming more frenzied.
"Wai-Iu-Eig-Wai! Wai-Iu-Eig-Wai! Wai-Iu-Eig-Wai!"
He then took the chicken and opened its stomach, cutting out the heart and liver. These too he lifted up and then ate. He felt power surge through him as he started to shake and dance in a frantic, frenzied motion. He spun around and around, his chant becoming louder and louder.
"WAI-IU-EIG-WAI! WAI-IU-EIG-WAI! WAI-IU-EIG-WAI!"
He saw his body surrounded by a grey mist. There were fingers wrapped around him. He kept spinning around and around until he convulsed to the ground, blood and gore oozing from his mouth.
When Nasi awoke, he could not remember all that had occurred. He could only remember the thick, grey tentacles flowing from his body and he knew he now possessed a stronger magic. He decided he would not perform his dark magic today, but he felt confident that in the near future, his dark spells would grow even stronger and he would need all his power to destroy Eigara. For many weeks, Nasi returned to the same altar and performed his ritual,

until one day he knew it was time. The tentacles of grey mist had now become thick and black. His body changed with each ritual. His skin became darker. His shoulder length hair became dry and brittle and his teeth began to turn black.

One day when he had completed his sacrifice, instead of burying the chicken corpse, as the meat had now become taboo and could not be eaten, he cut the bone out of one of its legs. He then proceeded to gather some of his stored magical substances. These he mixed in a bowl with some of the blood from the chicken. He then lifted the bowl up, imitating again what he had seen the missionaries do in their services, and drank it, always chanting his magic spell over and over again. He took the bone of the chicken, pointed it towards the Eilu village and conjured the image of Eigara in his mind. The bone had the same black, misty tentacles flowing from it. He drove the bone into the stomach of his image of Eigara to release her magic power from within her and make her weak. He twisted the bone again and again, making the hole in her stomach bigger. Each twist was more vicious than the last, until he felt he had killed her. All the while, he danced and twirled in a frenzy. His face was contorted and his eyes had turn upwards until only their whites could be seen. Then he collapsed convulsing onto the ground.

In her village, Eigara suddenly stopped weaving her basket. She had woven baskets since she was a small girl and could perform the operation without concentrating on the task. She felt herself becoming faint and fighting to breathe. Something was choking her and her hands lifted to her throat. Rihani, who had been talking with

Ema, felt herself grow cold. She dropped the coconuts they had gathered and raced towards her mother's hut. Something was terribly wrong. As she entered the hut, she was horrified to see Eigara struggling to loosen a noose around her neck. The noose was not made of twine, but a grey smoke-like substance. Frantically, she knelt down in front of her, trying to control her trembling hands. She worked quickly to unravel the woven fibre, but the more she pulled at the strands, the more difficult the task seem to become. Her shaking hands did not help. Rihani was desperate. She could see her mother's strength waning as she gasped for air. Rihani silently invoked her ancestors as she untangled the complicated strands, until finally she could pull them free. Rihani and her mother embraced, both in tears. Without words, both knew Eigara was in danger.

Nasi lay on the ground all night. The next morning, when he woke up, he knew that Eigara would die and that he, Nasi, would be the greatest sorcerer the island have ever known. His enemies would be afraid of him, for he was able to kill a great sorceress.

"People will know of my great power. They will bow before me or I will destroy them too," he smiled wickedly. Then a fleeting image of a young girl appeared in his mind. "Rhani?" He laughed louder and louder, until his laughter became a shriek.

Chapter Eighteen
Rite of Passage

Rihani and her mother never mentioned this episode again, however, both women had no doubts that Eigara was in danger. According to the island's traditions, Rihani had reached womanhood. Unlike the celebration given for most of the girls on the island when they reached this stage, Rihani's celebration would also be her initiation ceremony as a sorceress. A special hut was built for her near her parents and she would stay within this hut for almost three months. Rihani loved being in her hut and felt the happiest she had been since the sighting of the fire in the sky. She would now be considered a woman, and parents from other tribes would ask her parents if she would become betrothed to their sons. She knew her parents would favour someone such as Akua from the elite Ramoide class. However, like most of her generation, class distinctions were becoming less important to her.

Rihani thought about the young men on the island. Akua was her friend and the most likely candidate. But every time she thought of him or one of the other men, two blue eyes would appear over the image of the man. The dream she had seen of the future when Avery was sick still bothered her. She had gone over and over in her mind the reasons why she could not marry him. That is if even Avery wanted her, for he had been avoiding her since he recovered from his illness. They sometimes still met. However, he always seemed angry with her. She had to admit that she often hid now when he was coming her way, or turned in another direction, although she herself often spied him when he was unaware she was nearby. Avery was confusing and brought out strange feelings in her, so she did not want to think about him. Her life belonged to her people and she knew she would eventually marry someone worthy of her powers. She also knew that Avery would never truly understand her or her people. He now had a guardian, but she would soon be above his simple understanding of their world. She must marry one of her own people.

Akua had been staying in Rihani's village as he was expecting to marry Rihani. Both sets of parents had agreed that they were in favour. The day of the great celebration of Rihani's womanhood and place as a sorceress was approaching. He wanted to be near her. Rihani, meanwhile, spent her days between being educated in the secrets of family life, marriage and childbirth. She was not too concerned about the marriage part, for she knew this would not happen for a few more years, but the thought of childbirth was frightening as many women died giving birth.

She had already participated in some of the rites and ceremonies of childbirth. When a woman first believed she was pregnant, she would tell her mother and then her husband would be told. There were many taboos during this period in a woman's life. A special mat would be woven for the woman and this mat would be part of a spiritual ceremony in which the women of the village would gather around the mat in a circle and chant sacred words. The women would place their mouths close to the mat so the enchanted words would enter into it. The pregnant woman would also be fed specially prepared food, as was the case with the rites of puberty. When the baby was born, both the mother and a special sorceress would help the child into the world then cut the umbilical cord. The baby was washed with seawater. Mother and child would be given a little seawater to drink, as the sea was the very heart of their culture. Messengers were then sent around the island and great joy would spread amongst all the clans, with wrestling matches, dancing, singing all over the island.

Such things were for the future, however. For now, Rihani enjoyed her time being spoilt. She did not have to do any work and her body was massaged every day with sweet smelling coconut oil. Her friends who visited brought her fresh flowers every day, and they would make garlands. The girls spent a lot of time combing each other's hair as they laughed and joked. They sang songs as they wove mats and caskets, and threaded pretty shells through a fine string, making the gifts that would be given to guests at her celebration. It was custom on such occasions not only to receive gifts, but also to give each family a gift in return to mark the occasion. The girls also played string figures. They made intricate figures and chanted a story for each new figure. The food Rihani ate during this time was also special and prepared only for her. Rihani felt so happy. This would be a time to remember, she often thought to herself.

At the end of the three months, Aio invited the entire island to participate in the great celebration. Rihani was inside her hut with her mother and some of the women of their village. She knew what was about to occur and was very excited, although she knew that it would also involve some pain. Eigara sat next to her daughter and beckoned her to lie down on her mat. She started chanting a sacred song whilst the women prepared soot and sacred tools made from shells. Rihani's mother used these to tattoo on her daughter's face the beautiful markings that would identify her as a sorceress. Eigara then fastened a sacred bone necklace around her neck. Rihani had been preparing most of her life for this moment and she relished every detail.

Eigara also took a beautiful shell necklace from a small casket. Rihani looked at the necklace in awe for she recognised as the one the girl in her dreams wore. It was Ekewane's. The necklace had been handed down from mother to oldest daughter since the time Ekewane had lived. The small beautiful shells had been rethreaded throughout the years, but the necklace was still as beautiful now as it was then. Rihani was almost too afraid to touch it. Ekewane was her favourite ancestor and Rihani was afraid that if she wore it, the power of the necklace would be too great for her weak body. All the guests in attendance at the great celebration would know that she wore the famous necklace. She suddenly realised the expectations that would be was placed on her and her fears returned.

That night, Rihani dressed in a grass skirt finer than the one she usually wore. Around her waist hung a beautiful belt made of small shells and frigate bird feathers. The black feathers of the belt indicated that she was the daughter of a chief. Around her head, she wore a garland of sweet smelling frangipani and hibiscus flowers, and perfumed coconut oil was combed through her hair to make it gleam. On this great occasion, Aio wore his shell armband with even greater pride. His was the most powerful family on the island and he wanted to show their status. He also wore an elaborate necklace made of frigate bird feathers and this too was a symbol of great power.

The feast in honour of Rihani would be very elaborate and Aio knew the people on the island would talk about it for a long time. His older brother Polu, chief of the U'ulu, had bought milkfish, which was a special delicacy from the inland lake, and mango from the tall trees which surrounded the lake. At the celebration, Rihani was excited, overwhelmed. She glowed with happiness. Four young men carried her on a platform around a large fire. All the guests were laughing and singing as she sat smiling down from her perch. Rihani had never felt this happy before. She was now a woman and a sorceress. Her platform was lowered to the ground near her parents and, as if at a signal, the young girls started to dance. The drums boomed louder and louder as the tempo became almost frenetic and the girls danced to the ever-increasing rhythm. Rihani felt dizzy with excitement. On this day they were dancing for her.

She looked around and saw Avery. He was sitting next to her parents and smiling. Her heart beat even faster, in time with the drums. But when their eyes locked, he sadly lowered his head and Rihani felt a sharp pain in her chest. For a moment the happiness she felt faded. But then she was once again caught up in the singing and dancing around her. Akua pulled her up and they joined in the dancing. She was lost in the magic of the music.

Avery had never seen Rihani look so beautiful. The tattoos added mystery to her beautiful face and he thought, "If only I had the courage to ask her parents if she would marry me, but she is too far above me and will marry a chief's son. Her parents seem to favour Akua. How can I compare?" Avery could see the young men of the island flirting with Rihani. He knew that one of them would soon become engaged to her and had never felt so angry and jealous. All his life he had been a victim, and even here on this island he was no one. He did not belong. He fought the urge to get up and hit Akua or any of the other men looking at Rihani.

"I wish more and more I was back on the ship!" he thought angrily. He felt a strong urge to hit out, but instead quickly got up and hurried away. He needed to be by himself before his suppressed anger could no longer be contained. Unshed tears stung his eyes as his nails cut into his clenched hands.

Gadiya looked at his sister Rihani and smiled, for she was very beautiful. He had had his celebration into manhood a few wet seasons before and was now engaged to Adera. In a few more seasons, they would marry. Gadiya remembered his initiation ceremony. He had stayed in a hut with other boys his age where they were taught to wrestle and box, as well as the duties and responsibilities they would have towards their future wives and children. He looked at Ema, dancing with the other girls, and thought, "She will have her celebration in the next wet season."

Gadiya nudged Itu and they both got up and joined the dancers. The dancing and singing went on until late that night, then everyone returned to their huts to sleep. Those who had come from other villages around the island lay their mats down beside the fire and went to sleep. The celebration had indeed been worthy of Aio and Eigara's status on the island.

The next morning, Rihani got up early. She needed to speak to her parents and it could not wait. It was important. Her parents were still in their hut, so she called out to them. She entered the hut and sat down beside them. She hesitated and took a deep breath. She had to speak to them.

Chapter Nineteen
The Wet Season

Tamed noddy birds in front of huts

Torrential rain fell all night. At last the wet season had arrived on the island. People around the island were grateful to their gods and gave many offerings, for there would be no drought this year and there would be plenty of fish in the sea, along with coconuts, mango and pandanas, as well as taro and yams. The morning after Rihani's celebration the women and small children all headed towards their gardens. With them were several tethered sows. The pigs were very important for the Islanders as a source of meat, and they were also used in celebrations and were a sign of wealth. However, the pigs were also valuable for their gardening, for they would dig the ground, eating old roots and at the same time fertilising the soil.

The women and children dug with sticks and planted some of the taro and yams left over from the last harvest. Some of the bulbs had been left in the ground from last season and they would grow with the rain. But more patches for new plants needed to be cleared and so they set about making spaces around the village with the help of the pigs. The planting and clearing would continue for several weeks, and while the women worked in their gardens, the men went up onto the dark mountain where the tomano tree grew high up. The hard wood from this great tree would be used for building canoes, carving fish hooks, making spears and for other items needed in their daily lives. While they were high up on the mountain, the men hunted for noddy birds. Some of these birds would be eaten, whilst others were tamed and kept as pets on roosts in front of the villagers' huts. Only the chiefs could keep frigate birds, so the other men on the island were contented with the noddy birds.

Eigara, like all the sorcerers on the island, performed rituals and prayed to the gods and ancestors for bountiful harvests. They sacrificed chickens and used their blood to wet the soil. The blood was a sign of death and the rains would bring new life to the place where death had been.

This was the first time Rihani could perform the sacred rituals. Before, she could only help her mother. She stood before the plots of land that would be planted and chanted her sacred prayer. Seawater was sprinkled over the earth. This too was a sign of new life. When Rihani completed her rituals, she returned to the village and made offerings of yams and taro on the stone altar. There she met Eigara and Ema who had worked magic on other plots of land. Together they stood side by side, chanting their invocations.

They then entered Eigara's hut and continued to chant their sacred prayer. Rihani, like her mother and Ema, swayed backwards and forwards, letting the soothing tune take them into a dreamlike state. Rihani felt the strange, familiar feeling possessing her and the world around her became hazy. She felt herself become lighter and lighter until she was floating. She could see herself still swaying and chanting below and looked at her mother and Ema, who too were lost in their own worlds.

Rihani felt her body float outside her parents' hut and fly high up into the sky. For a while she hovered over her village. The images at first looked a bit hazy, as if in a dream, but she could still distinguish the objects below her. There was a white bird circling a hut. White terns circling a woman's hut were seen as a message from the spirit world that the woman who lived there was pregnant. "Raini is finally pregnant. Now we will have the sacred ceremonial blessing of the mat she will wear during her pregnancy," smiled Rihani. The oncoming birth of a child was a special time and everyone prayed for the health of both mother and baby.

High up into the sky Rihani soared, looking down on her beautiful green island. She could see the never-ending expanse of the shimmering blue sea. "I feel so happy to be so free!" she shouted to the birds flying around her. Flying was pure bliss. Her body was no longer tied to the earth below. Nothing could touch her up here and for a while, she let the breeze take her around the island like a feather in the wind. "It would be so easy to live up here and not return to the ground," she thought. Then the image of two blue eyes slipped into her mind and she sighed.

The mountain caught her curiosity. She wanted to see the top, as no woman had ever been there and she was curious. She also wanted to see Avery. Up here, everything seemed easier. She had stayed away from him but she also missed him. Avery still avoided being alone with her too. Since her initiation ceremony, she had spent most of her spare time with Akau. She had known him all her life and enjoyed spending time with him.

No sooner had the thought of the mountain entered her mind than she found herself floating towards it. When she flew over the top of it, she saw a large crater. The crater was green inside, but the shrubs and trees there were very small compared to those in the surrounding area. She felt a strong, hot current flowing up towards her and shuddered. "No wonder we are not allowed up here. There are strange spirits down in the hole. I can feel them," she thought.

Rihani looked at the tall tomano trees. There were many men cutting down large branches or carving out the canoes. Everyone was laughing and having a good time. She spotted Avery with Gadiya and Itu, and felt compelled

to call out his name. She was surprised when his head

turned up and looked at her. "Surely he can't see me?" she asked confused. Avery had felt a strange sensation. The hairs on the back of his neck stood up and he shivered. He thought he had heard Rihani call out to him. "It is only the wind," he thought sadly.

Avery went with Aio, Gadiya, Itu, and some of the other men high up onto the mountain. Avery felt apprehensive as he made his way through the hot, steamy undergrowth. There was no breeze and the humidity was even higher because of the rain. There was something sinister about the mountain, although he could not explain what it was. He noted that all the men were more sombre and often looked around cautiously. "I'm not the only one, then, who feels these strange sensations as we climb higher and higher up this mountain," he thought.

Gadiya and Itu joked about all the birds they would catch and the new canoe they would cut out from the tomano tree, but Avery could see on their faces that they too were not completely at ease. He could not stop thinking about Rihani and wondering what she was she doing now. He could picture her singing whilst digging the vegetable plots and planting the crops. He missed her already and dreamt about her every night. He stayed away from her and only looked at her when she was unaware of his gaze. He hated seeing her laughing and joking with Akau, but could do nothing. "There is no hope for me," Avery sighed sadly.

Avery was soon caught up with the activities of the men around him. He tried to catch noddy birds and at first he was not successful, for he had to snag them with nets on long poles and the poles were difficult to handle. But as the days went by, he became more proficient and could catch some. At night the men would roast the birds on sticks over the fire. After a diet that mainly consisted of fish and vegetables for most of the year, they tasted delicious. "Like chicken and fish together," he told the men when he had taken his first bite. The men laughed and joked, and for a moment, Avery felt his life was nearly perfect. "If only I could really be one of them," he thought.

"Rihani! Rihani! You must come back," Eigara called to her daughter. Rihani suddenly woke up and found her mother and Ema looking anxiously.

"You left us for too long. You must not stay away for so long or your body will not take you back!" explained her mother.

"I felt so happy and free," whispered Rihani. "Do you also fly?" she asked her mother.

"I have a few times, when I was is a deep trance. For your spirit to leave your body, you need a strong emotion like love, hate or fear," her mother explained. "But you must be very careful, for you can forget to return for a long time and by then your body will not know you."

Rihani nodded and sat there remembering the wonderful feeling she had just experienced. She understood her mother's words. She had not wanted to return.

The men stayed away for two weeks and then slowly came down the mountain with their canoes and noddy birds. Avery was anxious to see Rihani. He had missed her and wanted to tell her about his experience on the mountain, but knew he would only do so in his mind. The women and children could hear the men coming down the mountainside. Their loud laughter was carried down to the village. As soon as the women and children heard them, they ran out to meet them. Everyone was excited. Tonight there would be great celebrations across the island.

Avery recognised Rihani from a distance. As she ran smiling towards them, Avery thought to himself that she was taller than the other girls and more beautiful. Rihani eyed Avery shyly and then turned away. However, he had seen the strange look she gave him. "I feel so confused when it comes to Rihani," he sighed.

After their meeting, the men and the women returned to work to prepare for the great feast. The young girls stayed all day in their huts, preparing themselves. They combed each other's hair with coconut oil to make it shiny, threaded flowers to make garlands to wear around their heads and necks, and prepared their soft grass skirts. That night a large fire was built on the reef. When everyone had finished eating, there was a hush. A wave of expectation and excitement filled the air. Then the drums started beating. At first they were beating slowly and softly, but then the rhythm started building up. The drums beat faster and faster, until everyone in chorus yelled out. From off to one side, the young girls came in dancing. Their bodies gleamed as the firelight flickered and illuminated them.

The girls gently swayed, their grass skirts rolling backwards and forwards like the waves on the shore. Their arms also moved from side to side in gentle, flowing actions. They wore beautiful garlands around the necks and heads, and their long shiny hair swayed like soft waves. Avery was mesmerised. He held his breath as his heart beat in time with the accelerated rhythm of the drums. Rihani was smiling at him. The drums kept increasing their tempo and the girls also danced faster and faster, until it stopped. Everyone waited. Then the drums started pounding again, only this time they beat slower. The girls left the circle where they had been dancing and moved towards the boys.

Rihani danced towards Avery and beckoned him to join her. He could not dance so he sadly smiled at her, promising to himself that he would ask Gadiya and Itu to teach him. Rihani was still smiling at him as she approached Akau and they joined the other dancers. Avery felt devastated.

Chapter Twenty
Confrontation

The new religion spread slowly throughout the island. Only within the Eilu tribe did the influence seem less. The people of that village still believed in the power of their old gods and ancestors, and in Eigara as their powerful sorceress. She could speak to the spirit world and she would protect them. But slowly, the people on the island became sick again. This time, the sickness came from within.

First, the small children started to get sick. Their bodies were so hot they seemed to be burning. Many of the smaller, weaker children died. But then adults also started feeling unwell. They would lie down listlessly on their mats and their bodies would become very hot. After a few days, they started having difficulty breathing. The rasping sound of the sick struggling to breathe could be heard in every village. Then they started coughing in a constant, and at times violent, chorus of coughs. The Islanders had never been inflicted with such coughs before, so the noise was frightening to those who were nearby. The coughing left the sick even more exhausted, too drained even to drink. Their coughing fits grew more frequent until they started coughing up blood.

The sick complained that an evil spirit possessed their body. They would give up trying to respond to those nursing them and praying for them beside their mats. Not even the sorcerers could do anything to help. The adults started dying and those who were not sick started to panic. "What evil spirit has made our people so sick again?" they asked themselves.

Eigara often left her village and travelled around the island trying to help her people. But none of her herbs or chants would work. Finally one night, she staggered home exhausted. The people of her clan were happy to see their sorceress back in the village. They felt safer with her near. But a few days after her return, she started to become ill herself. Rihani sat beside her mother and cried. She was not strong enough to fight this evil spirit alone. If her mother could not help the people who were dying, how would she, Rihani, do so?

Nasi became aware that Eigara had become ill like many of the other Islanders. "My ancestors are more powerful then Eigara's! I am the most powerful sorcerer on the island! I can destroy Eigara!" Nasi would boast as he walked around the village. The people of his village were becoming afraid of him and tried to avoid him. If he had this power over Eigara, they themselves could have no power against him.

Rihani and Ema knelt beside their mother, softly chanting. They were unsure what spell to use. All Rihani could think of was Ekewane. Surely her spirit could help. So the two sisters prayed to their ancestor Ekewane for help. The days passed and Eigara's condition grew worse. She was dying. Rihani felt exhausted, as she had not slept for many nights. She left her father and sister beside Eigara and walked along the beach away from the village.

She proceeded along the shoreline and noticed the limestone bench nestled amongst the undergrowth. She crawled under the overhanging branches until she reached the carved-out seat. There she sat. Away from everyone, she let her despair and hopelessness come out. The tears ran down her face in a torrent and she let them flow. She put her face in her hands as great sobs shook her body. "I am a sorceress but I cannot save my mother," she wept.

She cried and cried, and then she felt a presence sitting beside her. A gentle hand was on her shoulder. Startled, she quickly turned to see who was sitting next to her, but there was no one. Rihani started whispering the words of her sacred chant. As the repetitive words were sung, she felt lightheaded. Again she felt a soft touch on her shoulder, and when she looked, there beside her was the girl of her prayers. The girl from the cave. Ekewane.

"Do not cry. You must be strong," whispered the girl.

"My mother is dying. Our people are dying. I cannot help them."

"You can help," replied the ethereal girl.

"I cannot," cried Rihani in despair. She sat there, still crying. She felt so hopeless. Her mother and her people depended on her, but she was weak and would not be able to help them. "I will disappoint my people. They are looking to me to take my mother's place. But I am not a strong sorceress like the other women of my family," she sobbed.

After a time, Rihani looked up. The ethereal girl had gone, but she heard the rustling of someone approaching her through the bushes. She gazed at where the rustling was coming from and saw two sad blue eyes looking at her through the branches.

"Avery!" she whispered.

Avery looked concerned as he sat down beside her. He did not know what to say so he just opened his arms and Rihani let herself be engulfed by his embrace. Rihani continued to cry and Avery only caressed her. She needed to cry, he thought. Then, when there were no more tears, she slowly lifted her face and looked at him.

"You are strong Rihani. You have great powers and only you can help your people," Avery murmured.

"I am not strong! I am not powerful! I cannot help my mother and my people," cried out Rihani.

"I did not believe in any magic before I came to your island. Now I have seen the power of your ancestors. I believe in you."

"But how can I help? I have prayed to our ancestors and our gods, but they do not listen to me."

"They will. But first, you must believe in your power."

Rihani and Avery sat embracing in their nook until they heard a loud commotion coming from the village. They stood up and ran towards the tumult. When they arrived, they saw Nasi standing in front of her mother's hut, surrounded by the whole tribe.

"I am the most powerful sorcerer that has ever lived!" boasted Nasi. "My ancestors are strong and I also have the power of the new God. Eigara's ancestors are weak!" He kicked the tombstone outside Eigara's hut.

Eigara could hear Nasi's boasts. Her fever had subsided a little and she tried to stand, but she felt too weak and dizzy. She could only lay there, listening and praying. Outside the hut, Aio looked stunned. The man standing in front of him looked psychotic. He knew Nasi. They had grown up in the same village and were members of the same tribe. This man did not even look like the boy he remembered.

"You have destroyed the resting place of Ekewane!" roared Aio.

Nasi looked at Aio for a moment, stunned. "Why is he so

angry? Doesn't he know I am freeing him from Eigara? She has cast a magic spell on him. That's why he married her! I am the only one who really cares about him. Now I am helping him. He must come back to our village now I am the most powerful sorcerer on the island," Nasi thought to himself, but he looked around uncertainly. All the villagers were looking at him. He could not back down now. Not now that his dream was coming true. He felt angry with Aio and laughed at him.

"You are blind!" he yelled. "Ekewane's spirit is weak. She cannot help Eigara or the people on the island. You must all bow down before me or I will destroy you as I am destroying Eigara!"

Nobody moved.

Rihani felt angry. She had never been this angry before. Nasi was killing her mother and he had violated the sacred tomb of Ekewane! She bowed her head in despair, and felt her body grow cold. In the distance the mountain screamed. Everyone stood paralysed as the scream tore through the village. Rihani started walking towards Nasi. The people, still shocked, silently parted, letting her through. When she reached him, she stopped and stared at him as if he were a strange creature.

Rihani started to tremble. She felt the cold travelling from her toes all the way up her body, leaving behind an icy trail. When it reached her stomach, she felt nauseated but the acrid bile did not escape through her mouth. As her body trembled, the world disappeared and in its place she could only see a red haze.

"Draw the mana from the world around you! Everything has power attached to it! You must bring this power into you!" she heard the mountain scream.

Rihani lifted her eyes to the sky. There she saw many red flames and she breathed them in. She could feel the fish in the sea and their life force. These too she drew into herself. She looked at the rocks, at the trees, at the insects. These were not objects to her now, but different sized red hazes. All of them, she took them into herself. She looked around at her people and saw they were all surrounded by a red light. Some appeared brighter than others. Her eyes caught sight of the brightest light of all, standing by itself. She looked closer and could see the form of the young, ethereal girl who had appear to her before. Ekewane smiled and lifted her hands to point at Rihani.

Rihani saw the form of Ekewane explode and burn into an intense heat. She could feel the heat from where she was standing. Whoosh! A ball of fire left the form and entered Rihani. She swayed with the impact. She could feel the heat burning throughout her body and the ice had now become fire. Rihani could look inside herself. She could now enter her own body. She saw the red blood surge faster and faster in her veins, carrying her along. She could hear a loud whistling as the air filled and then emptied from her lungs. Growing louder and louder was the pounding of her heart. It kept increasing in rhythm and volume. She covered her ears to muffle the booming sound. Her head could not endure the noise any longer. She wanted to scream but could not. She thought her head would explode and she would surely die. Then there was nothing.

Nasi looked at Rihani and laughed. "You are only a child

compared to me. You too must bow down in front of me." He turned and kicked another tombstone in front of her parents' house.

"NASI!" Rihani yelled. She glared at him with intense anger.

Nasi smiled and gloated. "Rihani! What do you think you can do to a great sorcerer like me?"

The mountain screams were ear-piercing. The people covered their ears in horror.

"NASI!" The voice that came from Rihani was strange, timeless. It could be heard above the screams coming from the mountain. Avery watched in trepidation. He wanted to go to Rihani and protect her. Maybe if Nasi cast a spell and he was standing in front of her, the spell would hit him instead? He tried to move, but it was as if the ground had taken hold of his body. He felt suspended in time. The people in the village felt the same strong hold. All looked just as petrified. The screams from the mountain suddenly stopped and an eerie silence surrounded the village.

Again the voice cried out, "NASI!"

Again, Nasi gloated. "Your ancestors are weak. My ancestors are stronger than yours. My gods are stronger!"

"NASI!" came the voice once more.

Nasi was beginning to feel taunted. He took the bone from his satchel and started chanting loudly, pointing the bone at Rihani as his body started trembling. His chant became more and more frenetic as the rhythm grew faster and faster. He felt dizzy, but still he twisted and turned, poking the bone in the direction of Rihani's stomach and heart. She stood her ground, glaring at him without blinking. He continued his frenzy until all he could hear was the pounding of his own heart growing louder and louder, then he collapsed to the ground in exhaustion.

Again the strange voice came from within Rihani. "NASI!" Avery looked at Rihani. Her body seemed to be surrounded by a strange haze.

"NASI, I do not see you. You have become a dark shadow. The shadow of evil surrounds you. You have betrayed our gods. You have betrayed your ancestors. You have destroyed what is sacred, the bones of our ancestors. Now your ancestors have turned from you. You have no family! You have no people! You have no ancestors! You have no gods! You will never join the spirits of your ancestors. Your spirit will wander. It will wander until time is no more."

Eigara, inside her hut, had heard Rihani and Nasi. She knew the voice coming from Rihani was from the spirit world. She was too weak to get up, so all she could do was pray that her daughter would be strong enough to survive the spirit that had entered her body.

Nasi looked at Rihani; a red haze surrounded her. He could feel a force radiating from her. He had difficulty standing up against it. He looked around, bewildered, and saw Aio and silently pleaded that his friend would come to his aid. Tears flowed from Nasi's eyes. He had not cried since he was a child. Back then someone had always comforted him. Now, however, Aio did not move and instead looked at Nasi with revulsion and hatred. He felt crushed. Abandoned. He fell to the ground. As he lay there paralysed and horrified, he felt his spirit leave him. He had betrayed his ancestors and his gods. Now he was only a shell. The people of the island stood still, unable to move, as Nasi crawled slowly away, a gaunt, shrivelled,

Maria Rigoni

defeated old man.

Rihani lifted her eyes upwards and fell to the ground. Released now from the grasp of the earth, Avery ran to her side. When he reached her, he cradled her for a few minutes, holding her close, protecting her. He lifted her listless body into his arms and carried her back to her hut. Akua also ran towards Rihani, but watched, appalled, as Avery picked Rihani up and carried her away. His fists clenched at his side. He wanted to rip Rihani away from him. "What right does this outsider have to carry Rihani to her hut?" he seethed under his breath. He decided to wait until Avery left the hut and there were fewer people around.

Aio also looked at Avery suspiciously. He looked around at his people still standing there staring at him and breathed out heavily. He wanted to be with his wife. Eigara needed him. As he entered their hut, he could hear soft murmurings. The villagers, waking from their hypnotic state, hurried away to their huts. Akua watched them scurry away and glanced at Rihani's hut. He was still very angry. He stormed away towards the reef. An eerie silence surrounded the deserted village, save for the distant mournful lament that could still be heard coming from the mountain.

Avery entered Rihani's hut and laid her on a mat. He did not know which mat was hers, for he had never been inside her hut before. Somehow, he was drawn to the mat at the far end of the hut. He gently laid her down on this as he looked around. From the outside, the girls' hut looked the same as the one he shared with Gadiya and his cousins, but inside was adorned with flowers and pretty shells. Near the mat where Rihani lay was a fine casket made from hibiscus leaves. The casket was delicately woven with the patterns of the clan. Avery knew these were the same patterns that had belonged to their ancestors and that they were jealously guarded by the clan. His familiar feeling of inadequacy was overwhelming.

He knelt down beside Rihani and caressed her forehead, willing her to wake up. He knew he should not have been the one to have picked her up and carried her away, but his actions were instinctive. "I will have to speak to Aio and Eigara. I know that they most likely not give me permission to marry Rihani, but I must try, for she has become part of me. But first, I must speak with Rihani," he thought.

Avery sighed. He stood and left Rihani's hut. He had to be alone to think. As he walked towards the reef, he felt a strong tug on his shoulder. He turned to receive a punch in his face.

"How dare you?" screamed Akua.

Avery did not answer. He had endured a lifetime of abuse and the hurt of so many years now finally came to a head. He retaliated with an anger he did not know he possessed and punched Akua in the stomach. The two men continued fighting and screaming at each other until the villagers in the nearby huts came out to investigate the commotion. When they realised who was fighting, they quickly ran to Aio.

"Aio! Aio come quick!" one of the villagers cried.

"Now what?" He went to see what all the commotion was about, thinking perhaps that Nasi had returned.

"Stop!" he roared when he saw the two men fighting.

They stopped instantly when they realised the voice belonged to Aio. Nobody disobeyed his word, even when they were in the midst of a heated fight.

"I do not want to know what this is about, but I have had enough anger for this night. Both of you go to your huts!"

Aio stomped back to his own hut where Eigara was waiting. He walked in and sat beside his wife. She had come back from the spirit world and would live. He picked up her limp hand and held it tight. Neither one of them spoke of Nasi. There was no need. Nor did they discuss the fight between Avery and Akau. They both guessed it was about Rihani.

Avery could not sleep as he was filled with too many emotions. He thought again that he would rather be back on the ship. At least there he did not have to think or feel anything, apart from fear, and he had learnt to adapt to that. He just needed to be smarter than the other men and hide when they were drunk. Here on the island, he felt confused. Sometimes he looked around the island and felt overjoyed, as if he were in paradise. But other times, like tonight, he felt so angry he wanted only to hit out.

"Rihani," Avery sighed. He cared about her and maybe even loved her. Rihani had been avoiding him as he had avoided her. She was different from the other girls on the island and it was this difference that he had difficulty with. She was a sorceress. He still felt uncomfortable with this, and tonight he had seen her power. She had been possessed, of this he was sure. He had been afraid of what he had seen and at the same time he wanted to protect her. It was when she fell to the ground that he could not stop himself. He needed to hold her and make sure she was alright. The same thing had happened before the encounter with Nasi. He had seen her leave the village distressed and wanted to go after her to help her overcome her grief. "What is happening to me? I am so confused," he whispered into the night.

Rihani awoke from a strange dream. Avery was still beside her holding her hand. The events that had occurred seemed unreal to her, but she knew it was she who had defeated Nasi. Now she understood. "My future will be difficult, for I am still weak. I have to control my emotions, and that will be very hard for me. I have the power to heal, but I also have the power to destroy. My mother's beautiful face changed when she was filled with anger and hatred. She condemned the violent white men and they had no escape. Did I look like her? Avery was there and so was Akua and the whole village. They would have witnessed me change. How can I face them again? I am not sure who I am now. Has my fight with Nasi changed me?" Rihani thought. But the question that occupied her mind the most was how would Avery feel about her now?

Chapter Twenty One
Joseph

Nasi disappeared. It was if he never existed. Most of the people on the island who had been converted to the new god no longer attended the services of the missionaries. Patrick and Joseph found themselves being ignored by the villagers. Nasi, who had been their prime leader in converting the Islanders, simply ceased to exist.

"We have to get the people to come back to our mission or we will have nothing," commented Patrick dryly.

"How can we do that?" asked Joseph looking up from his Bible. He needed to find a potent piece of scripture that would convince the people to return.

"We need to show them that God will punish those who do not believe in Him and do not attend our services," Patrick said.

The next Sunday, they did not hold any services, for no one would attend. Instead, they decided to go around the village to speak to the previously converted people and try to frighten them.

"You will die from a violent death and God will not have mercy on your soul. You are sinful people and must come back to the one true god. Come back and pray for forgiveness," the missionaries would repeat over and over. The people of the village were intimidated. "What if this God is cruel and punishes us? What will we do?" they asked each other.

By late afternoon, the missionaries were tired and hungry. They had exhausted all their supplies as the people no longer brought them food and gifts as they had done when they attended their services.

"We have to do something otherwise we will go hungry," Patrick stated solemnly.

Joseph, however, was dreaming as he often did of the chief's daughter, Ilia. She was young, beautiful and had often smiled at him. "If she was my wife I would be wealthy," he thought to himself.

"We will have to fish for ourselves," Joseph eventually replied, unperturbed. He had other plans in mind.

"There is a lot of food around the lake. The sea is too far and it's too hot to walk down and fish there. The lake is full of milkfish and the taro and yams are plentiful in the gardens. There are chickens and pigs roaming free. We could just take them. We will have to be careful as the lake is divided into sections belonging to the different families, same as the gardens are. We must go very early when it is still dark and everyone is asleep," continued Patrick.

As the weeks went by, the two missionaries resorted to stealing more food from the families. They would catch chickens during the night, as the birds were blind without the light of day. Then they would take them away from the village to a small cave where the men had set up a make-do camp to hide and cook their food. They also raided the gardens and took yams and taro. They would use their nets and catch the milkfish on the far side of the lake where there were no huts.

The two men became more daring as time went by. They now sneaked into huts when the occupants were not around and rummaged through their precious shells and shark teeth. These items were sought after to make necklaces and belts on all of the islands. Some shells were also highly valued for they contained spiritual powers and were used in ceremonial rites. Such precious shells had become a form of currency when trading with some of the ships that stopped at the island. The people in the village started to notice food was being pilfered from their garden plots. Others noticed that some of their precious shells and shark teeth went missing also, so they started accusing one another.

The two missionaries became aware of the unrest that their stealing had caused. They felt safe in the knowledge that the Islanders often argued over their possessions, accusing one another of being jealous of bigger yams or taro roots or precious shells, so they continued to steal without being overly concerned.

"As long as we are careful we will not be caught," they would often repeat to themselves.

Chief Polu became tired of the squabbling and sent for Head Chief Aio to see if he could bring peace before the arguments became violent. Aio arrived and held a meeting with the entire village. They were, after all, part of his family, as he had grown up in the village. He listened to all the complaints and said, "We do not know who is stealing so we cannot accuse another. It seems as if many huts have been stolen from. You must keep watch and see who is guilty. Polu, this is the first time so many things have been taken. You must put a guard around the village. I say this to you all: if a person is caught stealing from others, they will be banished from the island."

Aio knew that no islander would want to leave the island for this was their home. They also knew that the ocean was perilous and they would have very little hope of surviving such banishment. Joseph and Patrick snickered when they heard Aio's threat; for no one had thought it was them. As they became greedier and bolder, they started going to other villages nearby and pilfering through the huts there. They had decided that when the next ship stopped, they would leave with the valuables. They were becoming more selective and cunning. They would go into the gardens and only take a little from each one and they would only take the most precious shells and teeth.

"Tomorrow, we will go to the Arem village. It is far away so we will sleep near the village and wait," said Patrick.

"No, I have other things to do tomorrow," Joseph replied slyly.

Patrick did not ask what was more important than accumulating more treasure. He decided instead to stay in the village and again try to convince the people to return to the mission. It was still dark when Joseph silently crept to the back of the chief's daughter's hut. Ilia shared this hut with some of the other girls of the village. He had to wait. He would follow her, hoping she would soon leave the hut by herself. When the sun started to rise, the villagers started arousing. Ilia left her hut as she did every morning. She followed the trail around the lake to the place where she would bathe. Joseph followed silently, creeping through the undergrowth so he could not be seen. At one stage, Ilia turned around. The small hair on the back of her neck had stiffened, but she could see no one and there was no danger from any of the Islanders, so she felt silly. In the distance, she could hear the piercing cries of the mountain spirits, and again she stopped. Ilia had a strange presentiment, but shook it off.

"I'm a woman and no longer a child, and there is no danger on the island," she whispered to herself. Still, she had an uneasy feeling.

Ilia always enjoyed her early morning swim in the lake. She had discovered a small enclave that was hidden from anyone walking nearby. She loved the freedom of swimming in the small, sheltered part of the lake. She often took her empty coconuts shells and filled them with water from her special place. Upon arriving at her secret place, she took off her grass skirt and glided into the water. The cool water surrounded her. She felt peace in the tranquillity of the isolated nook. She swam around, enjoying the sense of freedom the water gave her. When she swam close to shore, she washed her hair and ran her fingers through it to untangle it. She then slowly walked onto shore, her mind immersed in her plans for the day. When one of the missionaries stood up out of the scrub, she was startled and screamed.

The man walked towards her. She stood there naked, trying to cover herself. The man grabbed her and she screamed again.

Joseph tried to quieten her. "Don't scream. I want to marry you."

Ilia was terrified. She kept fighting the man off but he tightened his hold on her. Joseph became angry. He hit her to silence her, but Ilia became frantic, she kicked and scratched at him. This made Joseph even angrier.

"You wanted me, you smiled at me!" he screamed as he threw her to the ground.

Ilia kept screaming. Joseph began hitting her harder to quieten her down. He lost control and kept hitting her even after she lost consciousness. "You are like all the others! You think you are better than me!" he yelled. The pent up hurt and frustration of his childhood now surfaced. He lost control and started kicking her. When he finally realised Ilia was motionless, he panicked.

"I have killed her. Now the tribe will kill me if they know it was me. I killed the chief's daughter. We must leave the island. First, I must hide her body," he mumbled.

He dragged her as far as he could into the thick forest. Although Ilia was small, her weight became heavier the further he dragger her. The forest let no fresh air through and he felt the perspiration run down his body. He came to a small cave-like structure cut between the tall limestone pinnacles. There was a small hole here, just large enough to drag her body through. He gathered branches and covered the entrance. Then Joseph ran back to his hut, where he sat trembling in a dark corner. Not long after, Patrick walked in. He had caught some milkfish and had them hidden in a wrapped mat.

"What is wrong with you?"

"Nothing!" barked Joseph.

Patrick shook his shoulders and lifted up the milkfish. "Lunch!" he smiled.

Rihani shuddered. Something was wrong, she could feel it. She ran in search of her mother.

"Mother! Mother!" panted Rihani as soon as she reached her.

Eigara looked worried. Rihani was frightened.

"What has happened?" Eigara asked.

"Something is wrong. Something very bad has happened."

Rihani explained as tears ran down her face.

"What?" asked Eigara again, concerned at the state of her daughter.

"I do not know. I only feel a great pain inside me. Someone is hurt and suffering. Their spirit is leaving them." She trembled.

"We must find Aio," replied Eigara as she quickly looked around.

Aio was near the reef with some of the other men of their tribe.

"Aio! Aio!" cried Eigara.

Aio turned to see his wife and daughter running to him. "Something had happened. Again," he sighed wearily.

"Aio, Rihani felt someone is hurt and in great pain. Dying," explained Eigara.

"Who?" Aio looked at his daughter.

"I do not know," Rihani replied in sadness.

"I will send messages around the island. I do not think anyone is dying in our village. None of the men have gone out to sea today. It is too rough," Aio stated seriously.

Avery, standing nearby, listened to the conversation. Like the rest of the tribe, he had no doubt that what Rihani said was true. He wanted to go to Rihani and sooth her, but her mother held her in her arms, so he sadly walked away.

Chapter Twenty Two
Ilia

Ilia's friends went looking for her when she did not appear

that morning. The girls felt uneasy and went in search of Vatsui, her mother. They saw her fishing off the reef.

"Have you seen Ilia?"

Vatsui looked at the girls. Something was wrong, she could feel it. A sharp pain tore into the centre of her stomach. "No. Is she not with you?"

"We have looked everywhere for her. We cannot find her."

Vatsui dropped her fishing line and ran in search of her husband. Ilia would never leave the village by herself, as she always went everywhere with her friends. She knew something must have happened to her daughter.

"Polu! Polu! Have you seen our daughter?" she cried anxiously.

Polu had never seen his wife look so frightened. "What has happened?" Polu asked anxiously.

"Our daughter is missing. Just like the other girls when the beachcombers were on our island. I am afraid for her," Vatsui cried, her eyes now overflowing. Too many dark things had recently happened on their island

"Do not worry. Ilia must be somewhere in the village. We will find her."

"Maybe the spirits have taken her because Nasi was part of our tribe. They are punishing us!" she exclaimed, terrified.

"We will search for her. I will send messengers to all of the tribes around the island. Do not worry, we will find her." Polu tried to convince his wife and himself, but he too had a terrible feeling. All of these bad things must mean their gods were very angry.

Messengers were sent around the island with the news that Ilia was missing, but nobody had seen her. The chiefs of the other tribes headed to the lake to help look for her. Aio and Eigara went too, for Aio was not only the Head Chief, but also Polu's brother and so Ilia was his family. Rihani also insisted that she go with them. She understood now that the pain she felt was Ilia's. Her spirit was calling her.

Gadiya, Itu and Avery went with other members of their village. Avery had never been to the inland lake where the U'ulu tribe lived. Despite the seriousness of their task, he was excited. They travelled north around the coast, stopping at some of the villages along the shoreline to spread the news.

"Ilia has disappeared and we are going to look for her!"

More Islanders joined in the quest. By the time they reached the track where they would have to leave the sea and climb up to the lake, the group had become large. Most of the men and some of the women from the various villages followed. By nightfall, all the groups had reached the lake.

"Have you found Ilia?" asked Aio.

Polu sadly shook his head. Vatsui was crying and Eigara stepped forward and embraced her. As she did so, she closed her eyes and saw an image of Ilia. Rihani also saw the same image as her mother and looked at her, bewildered.

"Ilia is not dead, but she is badly hurt," stated Eigara. Rihani nodded unable to speak. Everyone around had heard Eigara's words. They continued to look at her anxiously for any other information.

"We must find her. Her body is weak and the spirits will soon take her if we do not hurry," continued Eigara .

People started murmuring amongst themselves. "Eigara speaks the truth. She knows. We must find Ilia."
"Did you see where she is?" asked Vatsui.
"No. I am sorry. I only saw her laying on the ground, hurt."
"We will search. Take torches. We must find her," ordered Polu.

The men began to make torches from dry coconut branches. Gadiya, Itu and Avery also made torches. "We shall travel around the lake," said Gadiya.
"We have already searched around the lake and also in the water, but we did not see anything," replied Polu.
"We will look again, Uncle. Then we will go further up the mountain."
Polu nodded as the three boys walked away. "Tonight will be a full moon. The light will help," thought Itu. He was tired after walking all day, but like everyone else, he was desperate to find Ilia.
Ilia was Gadiya's favourite cousin, almost like another sister to him. She was the same age as Ema and they always laughed when they were together. She was always happy and smiled at everyone. He had never heard her complaining or arguing like some of the other girls.
The three boys started walking around the lake. Avery was fascinated by the reflection of the moon on the dark water. They had gone a little distance when Itu said, "I am tired. We have walked all day. Can we sit and rest a little?"
Gadiya and Avery agreed that they too were worn out, so the three boys sat down to rest, each lost in his own thoughts. They were so exhausted after their long trek that they soon fell asleep. The sun was filtering through the trees when the boys finally awoke. They felt guilty, having

slept, but knew that they had been too tired to continue to search during the night. Besides, they thought, although the moon was bright, they could see better during the day. The boys decided to bathe in the lake. In their village, they would bathe every morning in the sea, but the sea was far away from here. They dived into the water, relishing its cold sweetness which was so unlike the salty, warm sea. They swam and dived. The sensation of being able to swim in the lake felt invigorating. When at last they got out, they lay on the ground each feeling a little guilty about having enjoyed their experience. Again, they were silent with their own thoughts.

Gadiya lay on his stomach to let his back dry under the rays of the sun that filtered through the palm branches. He was near the surrounding bushes and was looking at something strange. He felt something was amiss, but could not decide what it was.

"There is something not quite right here," he said, mainly to himself, but Itu and Avery both heard him. The two boys looked around but could not see anything unusual. Gadiya kept looking and trying to understand what had given him that curious sensation. Then he quickly turned and sat up. "It's too clean! Look. It looks like someone has swept the sand. There is not a single leaf lying on the ground and there are only our footprints! Let's look around for more clues."

His heart was beating fast as he quickly stood up and was joined by the other two boys. They looked scrupulously around the small sandy alcove but at first they could see nothing.

"Look!" cried Itu, as he pointed to a small bush.

Gadiya and Avery went over to Itu and looked at the bush.
"The leaf! Look! That dark spot. It is blood, I'm sure."
The boys examined the leaf and agreed.
"Let's have a better look around here to see if we can spot
any more drops of blood or any branches that have been
broken," said Gadiya seriously. He knew something was
wrong here. He felt it.
The boys spread out, looking for anything unusual.
"Over here!" yelled Avery. Itu and Gadiya ran over to him.
"See? Something has been dragged through here. There
are small branches torn and the leaves on the ground
have been disturbed."
The boys nodded in agreement. They carefully followed
the faint trail. Sometimes they would find a few drops of
blood on the rocks or leaves. They knew that they were
on the right track. They kept following it for a few hundred
meters and then it stopped.
"Now where? I can't see any more signs," said Avery.
"If someone was dragging Ilia, they may have carried her
from here. We may be close, so let's spread out and look
around," said Gadiya. The three boys went in different
directions, looking for any sign of someone being dragged
along the forest floor.
"HERE!" yelled Gadiya after only a few moments of
searching. He had come to a high wall of limestone
pinnacles and was about to go in a different direction
when he noticed a torn piece of coconut leaf. There were
no coconut trees overhead so it seemed strange to find a
piece of leaf there. When the other two boys arrived, he
pointed to the leaf on the ground.
"That is part of a grass skirt! We cannot go further ahead

up the pinnacles. We'll have to climb."

The boys started climbing up the high pinnacles. The sharp edges cut into their hands and feet. When they reached halfway up, they looked down the other side. There lay a small, lifeless body. Ilia was all curled up.

"ILIA!" yelled Gadiya.

"We have to get down to her. There must be another entrance!"

The boys carefully climbed down again and started to look around for an entry.

"Here!" yelled Avery.

The boys looked at a hole that would have been large enough to drag a body through. It was blocked with stones. The boys cleared away the entrance and crawled through.

"Ilia!" called Gadiya again as he reached her.

The other two boys joined him.

"Is she alive?" asked Itu.

"I think she is. She is very weak. Itu, find my uncle and parents. I am afraid to move her."

Itu bolted out of the small enclosure, yelling as he ran. "POLU! AIO! VATSUI! EIGARA! We have found her!"

The people of the village had not yet started the day's search as they returned to the village very late the night before. Everyone heard Itu's screaming and came running.

"Where is she?" asked Polu.

"She is hidden near the lake between high pinnacles. Gadiya thinks she is still alive, but is very weak."

"Show us the way," both Polu and Aio stated in unison.

A large group of people gathered together and started following Itu. Eigara picked up the casket containing her medicine and nodded to Rihani to follow her. They started chanting very softly. They would need all the mana they could gather, for they knew if their magic was not powerful enough, Ilia would die. Rihani prayed with her mother, but she felt strange.

Patrick and Joseph also heard the commotion. They heard what Itu had said and returned to their hut without exchanging a word. Once inside, Joseph started to panic, pacing back and forth.

"We have to leave the island. If Ilia is still alive she will tell them it was me. They will also search our hut and find our store of precious shells and teeth. They will kill us. We must leave now!"

Patrick understood the urgency to leave. He did not question his friend.

"We will go down to the sea and steal a canoe. We will find another island," Patrick said determinedly.

Both men knew the possibility of them arriving safely on another island was remote, but if they remained here they would surely be killed by the Islanders. They hastily packed their most prized possessions. They would need these when they landed on another island and claimed to be missionaries. They also packed their stolen goods. They were worth a lot and would make them wealthy. Once they had packed, they slipped out of their hut and crept into the bushes that surrounded the village. They slowly made their way down the hill, keeping away from the main track in case they met any Islander. When they were in sight of a village, they stopped.

"We will wait until nightfall when the people go to their huts to sleep," whispered Patrick.

So the two men sat beneath the bushes and waited. When the sun set over the horizon, a fire was lit and the Islanders sat around it telling stories. There was no laughter or joking this evening, for they were all concerned about Ilia. After only a short time, they all returned to their huts. Patrick and Joseph waited until the moon was high in the sky. They crept down to the shoreline and picked what they believed to be the sturdiest canoe. They put all their belongings into it.

"We must search the village for more food and water. We do not know how far the next island is. We must take as much as we can," whispered Joseph.

Soon the two missionaries were ready to leave. The canoe was filled with their personal belongings, and with the food and water they had stolen. Both men had lived all their lives on an island and were familiar with the sea.

"We are now rich, brother. We will set up a new mission on the next island," grinned Patrick, thinking of all the things they could trade with their hoard and the wives he could buy. Yet both men were fearful of their journey, for the sea was unpredictable. They would pray and felt sure that God would take them to safety. After all, they were His missionaries.

Itu and his party reached the enclave. They headed up the mountain to the place where they had found Ilia. After a short climb, Itu called out and Gadiya answered.

"How is Ilia? Is she still alive?"

"Yes, I think so. Her body is still firm."

Itu pointed to the small opening, indicating that he would

remain where he was for there was little room inside. At that moment, Avery crawled out to let the others enter whilst Gadiya waited, still unable to touch his cousin in case she was taboo. Polu crawled in first, then he helped Vatsui and Eigara enter. When all were inside, Polu held back Vatsui who wanted to hold her daughter.

"No!" cried Polu. "Eigara must look at her first and see if her mana is still alive."

Eigara knelt down beside Ilia and held her hand over her, not touching her body. She closed her eyes and chanted the sacred prayer to their ancestors. Her hands hovered over the body then she ran them gently over Ilia. She could feel the pain inside the young girl. Many of her bones were broken and she was badly cut and bruised. Tears ran down Eigara's face and she wondered what this lovely, gentle girl could have done to deserve such cruelty. Eigara looked at Polu. "We must take her back to the village, but we must be very careful."

Polu crawled back out of the small opening and gave orders for some of the men to build a stretcher. He told the remaining men to dig the opening to make it larger so they could pull the stretcher through. Meanwhile, Vatsui, who was kneeling next to her daughter, leaned across without touching her body and cried in loud fearful sobs. The construction of the stretcher and the expansion of the hole did not take very long as the men worked quickly. They knew Ilia's life depended on it. When everything was ready, they slid the stretcher through the hole. Aio and Polu carefully lifted her limp body onto the stretcher and started pushing it out of the opening. The men on the other side pulled and soon the stretcher was out in the opening. Aio, Polu, Vatsui, and Eigara followed.

Ilia's stretcher was lifted onto the shoulders of four of the men, including Aio and Polu. Slowly, carefully they carried her back to the village. Rihani did not move. She tried calling out, but no sound came from her mouth. Perspiration started running down her back and she began trembling. She tried to move but was held firmly in place. As she looked, horrified, she saw two black tentacles snake across from the darkness of the undergrowth and start pulling her deeper into the forest. Rihani felt trapped. She could do nothing for the force was too strong. All awareness of her surroundings vanished and she could only see the two thin tentacles wrapping around and pulling her.

Nobody noticed that Rihani was not present during the journey back to the village. Ilia's life was in danger. That was all people could think about. But when they reached the lake, Avery looked back to see where Rihani was. He could not see her. He did not want to alarm the others, so he doubled back. "She must be tired and walking slowly," he reasoned. When he reached the small enclave where Ilia had been found and saw no sign of Rihani, he was confused. "I did not pass her along the track. Where is she?"

"RIHANI! RIHANI!" yelled Avery, but around him was only silence. He looked around to see if he could see which way she had gone and noticed some tracks leading further into the forest. "Why would she go that way?" he wondered. "It leads further into the dense forest and up the mountain. Something is wrong! Rihani would not go away by herself. She is needed to help Eigara."

Avery wanted to return to the village and get Gadiya and Itu, but he knew that it would take too long. "I must follow her," he decided. He began to follow Rihani's tracks. They went deeper and deeper into the dense forest. The intertwining branches were so thick that the sun was unable to filter through. The forest was also hot and humid as no breeze could push through the dense canopy. Rihani's tracks were strange. It appeared like she was not walking but was dragging her feet.

"What happened to her? Something is very wrong. I can feel it. Why is it always her?" he whispered, feeling frustrated and frightened. Avery lost sense of time. He was tired and thirsty, but he was desperate to find her. "RIHANI! RIHANI! RIHANI!" he yelled every now and again. But his throat was dry and his voice had become hoarse. Finally, he stumbled through the tall, aerial roots of a banyan tree into an opening. Inside was very dark. He looked around and found himself in a naturally formed chamber with walls and ceiling made of dense trees and shrubs. It took a few moments for Avery to become accustomed to the darkness. Then he saw her.

"RIHANI!" he screamed

She was kneeling in front of a stone altar, but did not respond to his cry. Something was very wrong. He raced across and when he reached her, he fell to the ground and embraced her. "Rihani," he sighed. She did not acknowledge him. Avery began to panic. "At least she is alive and unhurt, for I cannot see any blood," he thought, somewhat relieved.

"Rihani?" he whispered again urgently. Again, she did not answer and seemed unaware of his presence. "Rihani! What is wrong?" he asked, becoming more frightened.

Rihani looked strange.

Avery began to panic. He shook her, but still she did not respond. Avery started to cry. Without thinking, he kissed her. He had never kissed anyone before and was not sure if he was doing it right. He felt a deep fear penetrate his heart. Rihani's body was cold, her eyes were vacant and her mind was not there. "I cannot lose you! Please come back," he cried. Without her, his life would be without any joy and meaning.

In her bottomless abyss, Rihani felt something warm touch her lips. Someone was breathing air into her body and she slowly came to the surface. She pulled away and looked stunned.

"Avery?" she whispered.

Avery felt a whooshing sensation as the air flowed back into his lungs. He could breathe again.

Rihani looked around, terrified. "It is here!" she cried.

"What is?"

"It is still here, watching me. It wants to enter my body. I must fight it." She trembled.

Avery looked around, confused. The small hairs on his body stood up. He felt cold. This place was dangerous. His eyes, now accustomed to the semi-darkness, looked around the strange space. He looked baffled as he noticed crosses. Lots and lots of crosses. They were big and small, tied to the surrounding trees. The stone altar in front of him was spattered with blood. Various containers were filled with foul smelling bones and plants. Avery shuddered. It was eerie.

"W-what i-is th-this place?" he stammered.

"An evil dark spirit lives here. It was waiting for me," murmured Rihani. "Can't you see it? I must fight it!

It wants me!"
"Why you?"
"It has been following me. Even at our village. It is Nasi. He will not let me go. I am afraid, Avery," whispered Rihani. She tried to remain conscious but the dark tentacles were too strong and she slid back down to the black abyss.

"Why?" Avery asked again, confused. He could feel something sinister here but could not understand what Rihani was saying. "Rihani, we must leave. Your parents will be worried about you. I do not like this place. We must leave," he stated. But Rihani had fallen again into a deep hypnotic state.

Avery did not know what to do. He would not leave her. The only thing for him to do was to carry her. He stood up, struggled and picked Rihani up. She lay listless in his arms. With some difficulty, he carried her out of the enclosure. He did not put her down but kept walking unsteadily back down the track. He felt a surge of vertigo, but knew he could not fail Rihani, so continued to walk down the track. When he finally reached the pinnacle enclave where Ilia had lain, he could go no further. Exhausted, he put Rihani down and sat down next to her, still holding her close. He was afraid that if he lost contact with her, she would leave and join her ancestors.

The people of the village were waiting for the men and Eigara to return. They parted when the stretcher was carried through the village to Ilia's hut. The men gently laid her on her mat and left the hut. It was now up to Eigara's magic to help her. Eigara turned to the people and said, "You must all pray at the tombs of your ancestors and at the sacred altar. You must give offerings to our gods."

She then entered the hut. Vatsui was beside her daughter. The tears were still running down her face, but now she cried silently. She had to believe in Eigara's magic powers for she was the most powerful sorceress who lived on the island. Eigara looked around to see where Rihani was. She was nowhere in sight. Although Eigara felt concerned, she could not leave Ilia. She knew that all of the villagers around the island were praying and making offerings to their gods. Yet Eigara also knew that before healing Ilia's cuts and bruises, she had to save her mana. She had to bring Ilia back from the land between this world and the spirit one.

She began to chant. "A la istu Eigara mi trou isi aia ivu. A la istu Eigara mi trou isi aia Kabilia. I am Eigara. I call upon the spirits of my ancestors to come to me. I am Eigara. I call upon the spirits of my ancestor Kabilia to come to me." Eigara chanted the same words over and over again, each time naming an ancestor and all the while rocking backwards and forwards in rhythm with the chant. Sometime during the long night, Vatsui fell into an exhausted sleep beside her daughter. The sun rose over the horizon and Eigara leaned over Ilia, still chanting. She caressed her forehead, then took some liquid from a small container, dipped her finger into it and spread it across Ilia's lips. Then she repeated her action, but also putting her finger smeared with the liquid into Ilia's mouth. Eigara repeated this action over and over, and each time a few more drops would trickle down Ilia's throat.

When she noticed Ilia lick her lips, Eigara smiled. Her ancestors had come to her during the long night and helped her work her magic. She knew that this healing would be handed down through the generations to come when she had joined the spirit world, for this was the way of her people. Vatsui woke up, startled, she had not wished to fall asleep, but the tension she had felt over the past day had exhausted her. Now she looked at Eigara, who was smiling.

"Ilia's spirit is strong and she has come back to us. Now we must help her body heal."

Eigara got up and walked out of the hut. She stretched and looked at her husband, who was still asleep on a mat beside the hut. Polu, Gadiya and Itu had also slept outside the hut. Eigara walked to the lake and there she partook of her morning ritual of cleansing and restoration. In her village, she would have used seawater, for the sea was their great giver of life, but here the water from the lake would have to do. She needed to restore the power within her. Eigara's body had been weakened by the magic she had used to help the young girl, but she knew she had to continue her work in order to heal her.

When she had completed her restorative ritual, she walked back to Ilia's hut. She would need all her powers to heal Ilia's body however, she was concerned about Rihani's whereabouts. She approached her husband and woke him.

"Aio, Aio, have you seen Rihani?" she whispered.

Aio, still drowsy, took a while to understand. "No. Is she not with you?" he asked, confused.

"No, I have not seen her since we found Ilia. You must look for her. I am concerned."

"I will ask Gadiya, Itu and Avery to come with me." Aio too felt a growing concern for his daughter. It was not like her to disappear, especially when she was needed.

Aio woke Gadiya and Itu. He noted Avery was not there. "Where is Avery?" he asked angrily.

The two boys shrugged. "Why?" they asked in unison.

"Rihani is missing. Avery also seems to be missing. We must find them," he stated.

The three men left the village and returned silently to where they had last seen Rihani and Avery. When they finally reached the pinnacles where Ilia was found, they saw Avery lying on the ground still holding Rihani.

"Rihani! Avery!" yelled Aio.

Avery woke up, startled. He had only wanted to rest but exhausted had consumed him.

Aio looked at Rihani. She did not respond and lay there motionless. "We must take her to Eigara!" ordered Aio. He picked up his daughter and hastily made his way back to the village.

Eigara returned to Ilia. Vatsui was still sitting beside her daughter. Eigara felt a sharp pain as her mind drifted to Rihani. Ilia would get better, but it would take a long time for she had been deeply wounded. Eigara nodded and walked back down to the lake. She felt Rihani's spirit was in danger. She was still alive, but something was very wrong. She sat down and invoked her ancestors to help again her. After a while Eigara, suddenly stopped her invocations. She felt her daughter nearby and so hurried back to the village. She stopped at the place where she knew the men would come out of the surrounding forest. Sure enough, a little while later Aio emerged, holding Rihani. Eigara caught her breath. Rihani was unconscious. Aio took his daughter to a nearby hut and laid her on a mat. Now only Eigara could help. "What has happened to our daughter? She has no wounds but does not wake or speak," said Aio.

Eigara caressed Rihani's face. "She is possessed by an evil spirit," she replied wearily.

"Will you be able to help her?" he asked, concerned.

"No. She must fight the darkness herself. I can only pray to our ancestors to give her strength," she sighed.

Aio nodded and left the hut. Only Eigara understood the spirit world. Like all the Islanders, he was afraid.

Chapter Twenty Three
The Betrothal

Rihani lay unconscious in the hut. Nobody entered this hut, for the villages knew a dark spirit possessed her. Only Eigara spent her days and nights beside her daughter. She had prepared a special potion of wild red berries which she had crushed into a paste and then used to paint Rihani's face and body with powerful drawings. Eigara walked around outside the hut, whispering strange incantations to ward off other dark spirits that could threaten her daughter even more. She knew only Rihani could fight the evil that had entered her body. All she could do was protect her from any other evil entities and pray that her daughter would be strong enough to survive. Eigara did not eat or sleep but remained in a hypnotic state throughout that night and all the following day. Rihani was still unconscious, and whilst she remained in this state, Eigara could not leave her.

Rihani herself felt strange. All she could see was darkness, as if she was in some sort of black hole or prison. She knew she had to find her way out, but could not see any light to follow or help her escape. She tried to call out for her mother, but deep down she knew such cries would be in vain. Intense feelings of helplessness were her only company. She felt confused and tried to remember what had happened.

"Where am I? Am I still in the cave? I am so tired and weak," she thought. She just wanted it all to end. Life for her had become so difficult, with her nightmares, the abduction in the cave, the pain of her people, Nasi . . . It was too much for her to bear. "I do not want to be a sorceress. It is a curse. I was vain. I believed I was better than the other girls on the island but I want to be like them. They are happy," she cried. She could feel herself being carried away. "Ekewane!" she cried. Tears of defeat flowed down her face. "Please help me. Please help me." Her perilous call for courage was her last act of despair as fearsome shapes and shadows floated around her in the lofty darkness.

Then a faint light appeared. She looked around her prison and could distinguish a long tunnel, going upwards. She looked up, confused. The flicker of a flame was above her. "How can I climb up?" she thought despondently. She called out to Ekewane again for help. With her eyes closed, she started chanting her own special prayer to Ekewane. Slowly, she felt if she was becoming disembodied as she floated upwards. Rihani opened her eyes, she saw the bodies of many people all looking at her. Some of them looked vaguely familiar. They had a strange pallor, not like the golden brown of her people and not like Avery when he first arrived. Somehow she realised these strange people were the spirits of her ancestors. They did not speak or smile, they just stared at her and some reached out to her. Rihani did not feel afraid for she had prayed to them all her life.

The shadows of her ancestors faded as she passed through a vivid moving tapestry of her life. She was a baby, then a small child. She saw the blue sea, her initiation ceremony and Avery. "Avery," she whispered. Her body was becoming heavier and she was afraid of falling back down to the black abyss. She heard a soft familiar chant from somewhere nearby. "Mother!" she murmured. Then she opened her eyes and looked into her mother's face.

The story of Eigara's power in saving Ilia's life spread throughout the island. She had once again proven to all that she was a great sorceress. The disappearance of Nasi and the two missionaries were never spoken of, for to speak their names would bring back their evil spirits. Rihani returned to their village and her traumatic event was also not spoken about. She knew that Nasi was dead yet his black spirit was still lurking on their island. Ilia too recovered, although now she walked with a slight limp. She told her parents of her attack by the missionary man but neither he nor his companion could not be found. The Islanders believed their gods had punished them, and they did not question any further. The wet season continued and the people on the island were busy sowing their vegetable gardens. The island had not returned to the normal quiet they had experienced in the past, for too many evil spirits still loomed in their memories. Still, the Islanders went about their daily lives. Every now and again, when the piercing screams could be heard coming from the mountain, they silently left what they were doing and returned to their villages.

Avery felt as if he was slowly becoming a true islander. He was learning to fish by using a throw-net and by diving off the reef for eels and octopus. The island was now his home and he loved the gentle people who lived on it. "They have accepted me as one them," he would smile to himself. From time to time, a ship would stop for supplies, but Aio never let anyone set foot on the island again. The Islanders were now suspicious of all strangers. They knew what goods the people on the ships wanted and would row out to meet them. Avery, as always, was an essential part of the trade as he could speak the language spoken by the crews on the ships.

He sometimes spoke to Rihani but they were never alone. He felt uncomfortable around her and she too looked uncomfortable in his presence. They each still avoided one another. But Rihani had become even more important to him and he needed to speak to her and see if she felt the same way. Avery was afraid. Her betrothal to Akau had not as yet been announced, so he knew he had to ask Aio and Eigara about marrying Rihani before it was too late. His experience when he found her after they had gone to find Ilia had given him hope. He still felt at times angry for no reason at all, but these instances were becoming less frequent. The ship and his past were now becoming only distant memories. He no longer wished to return there as he sometimes had before.

One morning, whilst Rihani and Ema were collecting water from the brackish pond, he followed them. When he caught up with them, he asked, "Ema, could I speak to Rihani alone, please?" Ema and Rihani smiled at one another and Ema continued walking whilst Avery shyly picked up her hand and lead her to a small, secluded nook near the track. There he found an old tree trunk to sit on, and he slowly beckoned her to sit beside him. Avery was very nervous, but he remembered the dream from the time when he was very sick and Rihani had looked after him, so he took a deep breath.

"Rihani. We must speak. I w-would like to marry you. I know I have no land and nor do I belong to the Ramaoide class. There are many young men who deserve you more than I, but . . . but I love you and I will always look after you. If you say yes, I will ask your parents if one day we could marry," Avery blurted out. He was stunned, as he had not planned to propose to her, but when he saw her, the words just seemed to come out of their own accord. He was embarrassed and too shy to look at her.

"Avery," she said softly. "Many things have happened to me and my people since the time of the fire in the sky. I fear our time of sorrows have not ended." Rihani looked around the surrounding undergrowth. It looked dark and menacing. She trembled. Something was still watching her. "I am a sorceress. If our people are to survive I must learn more. I have told my parents that I wish to marry no one just yet, but I too love you. If we survive, we will marry one day, so go to my parents." She smiled shyly.

Avery could not believe it. Rihani loved him. She loved him! He felt overjoyed and hugged her tight. His life had always been full of pain, but the joy he now felt made up for all the past hurt. He pulled back from his embrace and gave Rihani a bracelet made of tiny shells. It had taken him a very long time to find such tiny shells, drill small holes in each, and finally thread a fine string through them. Gadiya had taught him how this was done. It had him taken numerous attempts before he succeeded, especially drilling the holes without breaking the shells. Finally, though, he was satisfied with the delicate bracelet. He smiled shyly at her, took her hand and fastened the dainty bracelet around it.

Rihani's eyes filled with tears as she looked at it. "You must go now and speak to my parents, for I cannot wear this beautiful bracelet until they have given us permission to be betrothed." She smiled and ran to catch up with her sister.

Rihani had also been uncertain. Her dreams were confusing but she knew they would come about and she would marry Avery. She had argued with her parents on numerous occasions when they had come to her with the proposals of parents of many of the young men on the island. They were especially keen on Akua and continuously explained to her the reasons why she should marry him. But Rihani knew that her life was bound to her magic. She had seen Avery in her future from the beginning.

Avery was overjoyed, but he now had to face Rihani's parents. He knew he had nothing to offer except his love for her. He doubted this would be sufficient for them. Rihani seemed optimistic, however, so he had to gather his courage and prepare himself for a refusal. Rihani was the Head Chief's daughter and her mother was a great sorceress. One day Rihani would inherit most of the land and coconut trees belonging to her mother, as was the custom on the island. As if this was not enough, Rihani herself had already proven to be a great sorceress. One day all the people of the island would come to her for help. It was after yet another convict ship had stopped for supplies at the island that Avery knew that he must at least risk asking Rihani's parents for her hand in marriage. They would wait for a few years before the ceremony would take place, but in the meantime, if he was given permission, no other man would be able to propose to her. Avery saw Rihani's parents sitting by their hut and slowly approached them. Over the years since he arrived on the island, he had grown taller and had now a muscular build. His skin had become permanently tanned because of the constant sun. No longer was he the frightened, abused boy who had been saved by the Islanders. Instead, he had proven to himself and the Islanders that he had become an important member of the tribe. With these thoughts in mind, he gathered the courage to face Rihani's parents.

"Good morning Aio. Good morning Eigara. I have come to speak with you."

"Sit," indicated Aio.

Avery sat down near the couple and waited. He was in no hurry to speak; for he needed to be sure the words he used would be correct.

"I-I know I have no tribe but yours. I know I have no wealth and I am from another place, far away. I know I am not worthy, but I love your daughter and want to marry her."

Aio looked at Eigara and she nodded. For a long time the three sat there silently, each absorbed in their own thoughts.

Finally, Aio look at Avery and said, "What you say is correct. Rihani is our eldest daughter and will inherit much wealth. One day she will be a great sorceress. The people of the island will come to her for help when there is no other to help them. Rihani has seen her future and has refused to marry. In the past, she would have obeyed us in our choice for her husband, but the young are different now and we must accept this. We have spoken and know that you will care for our daughter. You have shown that you are important to us, for you can speak the language of the crew from the ships. So, if Rihani agrees, Eigara and I will give you permission to marry."

Avery could not believe his luck. He felt so emotional. Not only was he accepted as a member of the clan, but also now he could marry Rihani and finally have the family he never had. Avery was overwhelmed and could not speak. His eyes filled with tears. He had to leave before he started crying for they would think him weak. He resisted the tears with all his might, stood, nodded to Aio and Eigara, and raced to tell Rihani the news.

"He will make a good husband and father. It was he who found Rihani when she was lost to all. Our children are changing and we must accept the new," smiled Eigara.

News of the betrothal between Rihani and Avery spread throughout the island. They would have to wait a few more wet seasons before they could marry, but they did not mind. They spent all the time they could together. Rihani was still curious about the faraway lands and wonderful things Avery had seen. He told her about his past, and the squalor and suffering many people like him had to live with. Rihani's eyes filled with tears as Avery told her about his life before coming to the island.

Chapter Twenty Four
The Volcano

A growing rumble began in the deep bowels of the earth. A thunderous vibration accompanied a tremor that shook the island violently. People fell to the ground, unable to stand. The island was rocking from side to side as the whole place were a boat about to tip over. Everyone was too petrified to speak. They gazed open-eyed at the rise and fall of the ground beneath them. Some of the huts collapsed. Stone altars in the centres of the villages crumbled. Waves lifted high up into the sky and crashed down on the shoreline. Everything near the shore was carried back into the angry sea.

People on the ground started screaming. "Help us!" they cried out loud, although they were not sure to whom they called.

Aio stood up from where he had fallen and began yelling out orders. "RUN! RUN! Up to the mountain!"

The people groggily got up. When they comprehended Aio's words, they ran screaming. They did not ask questions. They just obeyed their Head Chief.

Avery looked for Rihani. He could not see her and prayed she had not been fishing, for those who had been on the reef had gone to the spirit world. "RIHANI! RIHANI!" he kept screaming as he ran towards her hut, praying that she was still alive.

People ran everywhere, trying to find their families. It was difficult to find anyone because of the chaos.

"RUN! RUN! Up to the mountain or we are all lost," screamed Aio again.

Everyone stopped, confused. Where should they run? Aio was standing, pointing to the mountain. Then all turned towards the mountain and ran, still screaming out in fear. Aio looked towards the sea and saw another wave, even bigger than the last approaching. He could not wait. He too had to run. They could all feel the wave. The air around them was being sucked back. Nobody looked behind them. They just ran and stumbled up the side of the mountain. The mountainside was very steep and their muscles screamed out in pain as they climbed. Their lungs were struggling to breathe. Still they ran, pulling those who were slower up behind them.

When they had climbed halfway up, they stopped. Some fell to the ground, exhausted, whilst others watched the approaching wave in horror. The ground beneath them shook again, and those who had remained standing dropped to the ground. Aio looked around to see if he could see his family. Eigara, Ema and Itu sat huddled together. Itu was holding a terrified Ema, trying to protect her. Her legs were bleeding from scratches, but she was alive. He looked around again, but could not see Gadiya, Adera, Rihani or Avery, and his heart sank.

Avery had finally managed to enter Rihani's hut. He was desperate. How could the gods be so cruel? Now that he finally found happiness, it would surely not be snatch away from him!

"RIHANI! RIHANI!" he screamed. The tears were now flowing down his face. He had to find her. His life would be nothing without her. Rihani lay on the floor in her hut were she had fallen. She looked up, confused, as Avery stooped down and gathered her in his arms.

"W-we must hurry and run to the mountain,"

he stammered, relieved to have found her.

Avery quickly picked her up and they ran outside. The earth beneath them was shaking again and Rihani fell. He picked her up and unsteadily ran, dragging Rihani behind him. He looked back at the approaching wave and saw Gadiya pulling Adera. They were to be married this coming season, but they were moving too slow and the oncoming wave was fast approaching them.

Gadiya had turned and run back when he noticed Adera had fallen and was not getting up again. It was difficult, for all the people were running in the opposite direction to him. Finally he reached her and bent down to help her up. Adera was crying and tried to get up, but her ankle would not hold her. Gadiya swept her up in his arms and ran towards the mountain. He could not run very fast because of the weight he was carrying. At one stage, he turned his head towards the sea and stopped. The monstrous wall of water was fast approaching. He felt the whipping wind slam into them and he looked down at Adera and closed his eyes, realising they would join the spirit world together. This was the last thought Gadiya had as he looked into Adera's eyes. The impact of the wave hit them with blinding force.

Avery could feel the sea spray on his back. He knew they could not run fast enough to escape the oncoming wave. He looked ahead and saw a tall limestone pinnacle. He pulled Rihani even faster until he reached a high point. He did not hesitate to grab hold of her and push her with all his strength up as high as he could. Then he too jumped up. The pinnacle had razor sharp edges that cut deep into their hands and feet, but still he scrambled higher and higher pulling Rihani with him.

The roar of the approaching wave was deafening. They had climbed almost to the top when he saw that the pinnacle branched into two narrow towers. He pushed the bleeding Rihani into the crack in the middle of the towers, and then followed her in. They barely fitted and the limestone's jagged edges cut into them like knives.

Avery held Rihani close and screamed, "HOLD ON AND HOLD YOUR BREATH!"

The great wave hit them. All they could feel was the swirling mass of water trying to pull them away from their precarious refuge. The water kept coming and coming. A wet dark spiralling mass surrounded them, pushing them even further into the sharp blades of the limestone. The water did not recede for a long time. They held their breath, though their lungs were now bursting. They knew that they had only moments left before they would drown.

Rihani thought about Ekewane, but she felt too dizzy to pray and her lungs felt like they would burst. Then the water started pulling back, taking everything in its path. Avery held onto Rihani and the pinnacle. The stone was cutting into his hands and the pain was excruciating. He felt as if his hands were being ripped open. The top of his head felt cooler. He gasped for air, hoping that the water had retreated enough, but his lungs filled with water and he started choking. The sea was withdrawing quickly and he spluttered out the water and gasped again for air. This time he felt his lungs expand as the air filled them. Rihani also gasped as her body went limp. She was exhausted.

Avery held her for a few more moments until

they could breathe more normally. Then he slowly pulled his hands away from the razor sharp pinnacles. They had been impaled by the limestone and were bleeding profusely. He looked at Rihani and, although her hands were not as seriously damaged as his, her body too was covered with cuts and scratches. Avery did not wait any longer out of fear that the massive wave would return again. He climbed down onto the soggy ground and helped Rihani descend. They gingerly continued to climb the mountain. Now that the roaring wave had become fainter, they could hear wailing and screaming ahead of them. They felt heartened by the sound. At least some of the villages had survived.

Aio sat down next to Eigara and embraced her. She too had realised that their children were missing.

"The wave would now be crashing over our village. No one who remained would be able to survive," Aio thought sadly.   Ema looked up at the two bloodied figures who were coming up the track and screamed, "Rihani! Avery!" Everyone followed her gaze and they gasped.

Rihani's family ran towards them and helped them until they reached the small clearing where the Islanders had sought refuge. Before anyone could speak, they heard the terrifying noise again as the angry roar echoed throughout the island. The people looked around, horrified. They thought their gods must be taking them all to the spirit world. When the thundering noise stopped, Aio walked towards the outer end of the small clearing and made his way out of the undergrowth. Then he saw it. Way out on the horizon, rising up from the Pacific Ocean, was a billowing cloud of smoke ascending into the sky.

A large fire was also visible beneath the smoke. Flames were being thrown high up into the sky, causing the sea to turn red as if it too was burning.

Some of people of the village were still screaming in fear. They either knelt or lay prostrated on the ground because they had nowhere else to run. The roaring noise and explosions continued to light up the island. The Islanders lay there all night, too afraid to move. The flickering fiery red reflection shimmered over the land and sea. The spirit of the mountain could be heard mourning its sad lament. The mountain that they had always been so wary of was now their refuge. The spirits of the mountain were protecting them. Only the children slept that night, as the adults were too afraid to sleep and too afraid to speak. They just lay there, invoking their ancestors and gods.

The long, terrifying night finally ended, but no sun appeared on the horizon. An eerie light shone weakly where the sun would normally have been. The explosions had finally stopped and all was deathly quiet. Even the red waves seemed to have ceased their crashing onto the shoreline. The people looked around to see everything covered in a thick grey dust. They could still see the fire on the horizon, spewing flames and thick billowing black smoke. Every now and again, they glanced up at their mountain. They could not see its top, but everything around them was bathed grey and red. The earth shook again, although less violently than the day before, and again they cried out to their gods to have pity on them.

All through the day they lay huddled together amid the strange red light that enveloped the island. Out on the horizon, crackling spurts of fire were still being thrown up into the air. The dark, burning shadow was still rising up from the sea. Rihani was lying on the ground where she had fallen when they had arrived at the make-do camp. Avery was still holding her, protecting her. He vowed he would not let her be alone again. The blood on their bodies had clotted and their cuts and scratches were swollen. Itu and Ema were sitting on the ground nearby, also looking around terrified.

"Gadiya? Adera? What has happened to them?" cried Ema.

Aio was sitting beside Eigara. She opened her eyes to see her husband looking at her. The loss of their son and Adera sat heavily in their hearts, but she knew that Aio and her people would depend on her more than ever before, for only she could tell their people what was happening. The smaller children had woken up and began to cry at the strange sight around them. Their parents soon hushed them and then they too sat silently in their parents' arms.

"What will we do?" they kept asking each other. They turned to Eiagara for help, for they knew that only their gods could cause such fires. The Islanders lay there for many hours, too afraid to stand up, but eventually Aio rose unsteadily. As Head Chief, it was his duty to lead his people, even though he too was terrified.

"We must go to the Iwa village. The lake is high up from the sea and it may have been saved. We must be brave and face the angry gods together. Other tribes who have survived will also be on the mountain and we must search for them," he stated loudly to his clan.

People started getting up, bewildered. Their

chief had spoken. Smoke continued to billow from the sea, although it was less than the previous day. Eigara bent her head and started chanting, and Rihani and Ema joined their mother in her prayers. Aio and some of the other men started collecting coconuts and other food.

"We must eat and drink or will die," Aio stated.

The next day, the tribe started walking towards the lake. Survivors from other villages also arrived at the lake. Now that they could face together what the gods had sent them, they felt a little braver. The Islanders built small fires around which they huddled and whispered. A strong, acrid smell filled the air, and the eerie red light still surrounded them. They could hear the soft, monotone chants of the sorcerers praying to their ancestors, and felt a little more hopeful. The camp was crowded, as all survivors were present. It had been the first time since ancient times that the whole island had gathered together.

Two days later, the Islanders could no longer see the fire on the sea. Only the dark shadow and smoke were present. A thick, murky cloud still shrouded the island like an eerily drawn out twilight. Finally, the Islanders turned to their sorcerers and asked, "Why is the sea burning? Why are the gods angry? What have we done to deserve their wrath? Will we all sink down to the gods of the sea and burn? The island tipped and we almost slid off it! What are we to do?" All of these questions were asked over and over again.

Aio knew that Eigara and his daughters had been calling the spirits of their ancestors, and he prayed that they had been answered. The Islanders gathered around a large fire. Eigara joined Aio, and Rihani sat next to Avery, placing her hand into his. Ema found her way to Itu who embraced her.

"Eigara! Why are our gods angry?" asked the people.

Eigara looked around at the other sorcerers and sorceresses. Sadly, she looked at her people and closed her eyes. She sat there swaying for a few moments and then lifted her head and replied, "This was a warning of what is to come. Our gods are angry. Our future children will no longer pray to their ancestors and our gods will be forgotten. Our magic will be lost, for our children will be ashamed of us. Our children will be lost. They will face grave problems and they will be confused, as they will not know who they are, for without the past there can be no future. They will turn to new gods, new values and different taboos. They will no longer care for the old, but will be overwhelmed by the new and will be ashamed of their past. Our children will become greedy and sell our sacred lands. Our home will no longer belong to our children, but to those who will exploit it."

Eigara's face was wet with tears for her people. She had lost her son to the spirit world. Many others present had also lost loved ones. The gods had started claiming their price. Everyone was solemn and started wailing. They did not doubt Eigara and they knew that what she had foretold would come to pass.

That night, Eigara and Aio sat quietly alone in a small shelter they had built. Outside the mist threaded through the makeshift huts. Eigara held Aio's hand. She looked at him sadly and said, "Our gods and the dark spirits have made our people suffer. But these evils are not the biggest dangers our people will face in the future. The biggest dangers will be silent. They will come without us understanding their perils. Our island will be home to many strangers." The wind whispered eerily outside the hut, as if to repeat Eigara's words.

"They will bring new gods and exciting new things that will make our people's lives seem easier. The people will accept these without understanding the perils they bring. Our island will be home to many strangers," she repeated. Outside, the whisper of the wind continued.

"But our children will pay a very high price for these things. They will change and lose their identity, their gods and their ancestors. They will be lost and we will not be able to help them, for they will forget us. Avery says there as many people beyond our island as there are stars in the sky. He says there is only pain out there, where those with power and riches do not share but exploit others. These people have many new things that our people want. Nasi believed in their God, so perhaps he is strong. Still, we must fight. We may lose, but we cannot just accept these coming dangers, for if we do, our gods will destroy us. But how can we survive when our gods are against us? Who will help us?"

The whisper faded amongst the mist that surrounded the grey mountain. Overhead, a white tern circled their hut.

Rihani watched the tern and smiled wearily. "A new life," she thought.

The white tern

Epilogue

Charity stood mesmerised in front of an ancient kula-ring armband displayed in the Melbourne Museum. This was her last day in Australia after seven years here. She had heard stories about shell armbands before, but had never actually seen one. She had always been fascinated by the stories of the kula-ring that were described in books when she was in high school. Now, coming face to face with such a relic gave her a feeling of déjà vu.

Her friends wandered along to look at other displays, but Charity could not bring herself to move. She had studied medicine at the University of Melbourne. The years away from home had been difficult and she often felt homesick, but tomorrow she was flying back to her home as a doctor to become part of the medical team in the small island hospital. The first part of the trip would take her to one of the larger islands where there was an airport. Then she would have to catch the twin-engine plane that could land on the small runway built by the Japanese soldiers during their occupation of her island. The plane only visited there once a week to bring mail, supplies and the occasional tourist.

She gazed again at the shell armband and looked to see its provenance. The information panel beside it said that it was found with the remains of a Japanese veteran of the Second World War but that its original provenance was unknown. Charity reflected that her island home had seen many changes over the years. During the First World War, it had been occupied by England, then in the Second World War by first the Japanese and later the Americans. The only income her island had was tourism, so a large hotel had been built on it. Tourists came to see the volcano, which had never erupted but regularly sent smoke rising high into the sky.

Young dancers often performed the hula for tourists, but Charity knew that these dances and songs were adopted from the other islands, for the people of her home did not remember their original chants and myths. They had been lost over time. The only history the people of her island knew was recent. It had started with the missionaries, who had kept fragmented records, and continued under the occupations of the different colonial powers. Charity sighed and wished the island had kept some of their past culture, but it had all been forgotten many generations ago.

Her friends had returned from their wanderings and stood beside her, wondering what was so fascinating about the shell armband. Charity turned and smiled at her companions. "They could never understand," she thought, as her striking blue eyes sparkled against her golden skin.

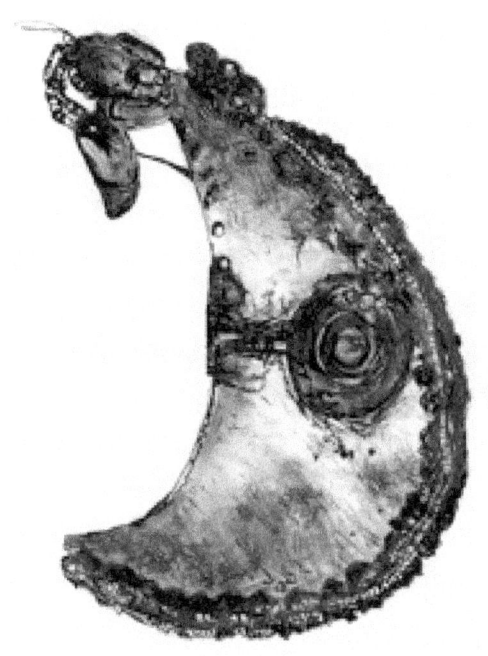

Shell armband

Tribal clans and classes

Book 1.
Ramaoide - elite members of the tribe

Eilu clan - descendants of the Great Head Chief Ekriaro, who remained on his island home
Original members of the tribe who settled on the new island
Erangue (father)
Emenear (mother)
Ekewane (girl, aged 12)
Enara (boy, aged 8)
Equi (boy, aged 4)

Book 2
Descendents of Ekewane and Emarr
Eigara (mother and sorceress)
Aio (father and chief of Eilu clan, as well as Head Chief of the island, originally from the U'ulu clan)
Gadiya (boy, aged 16)
Rihani (girl, aged 14 year)
Ema (girl, aged 13)
Adera (girl, aged 15, betrothed to Gadiya

Ramaoide (elite members of the tribe)
Yarle clan
Dara (chief)
Akau (boy, aged 16)
Kabaya (girl, aged 14, missing)

Enename (middle class members of the tribe)
Iwa clan

Original members of the tribe that settled on new island
Ramanmada (father)
Enemame (mother)
Ioopu (boy, aged 16, deceased)
Emet (girl, aged 14)
Iudi (girl, aged 14, Emet's cousin and friend)

Book 2
Descendents of Ramanmada and Enemame
Aio (married to Eigara, now chief of Eilu clan and Head
Chief of island)
Polu (chief of Iwa clan)
Vatsui (his wife)
Ilia (his daughter)
Nasi (sorcerer of the village)
Sitio (lower class members of the tribe)

Kalab clan
Roqua (father)
Gorube (mother)
Emmar (boy, aged 16)

Book 2
Erani (chief)
Iwi (young girl who disappeared)
Strangers from other places
Avery Jones (boy, aged 14, marooned on the island)
Captain of whaling ship, the Planter
Captain Fitzsimons Caine

Owen Pollack (convict and beachcomber)
Briggs Wright (convict and beachcomber)
Liam Petterson (convict and beachcomber)
Joseph (missionary from another island)
Patrick (missionary from another island)

<<<<>>>>

Tribal Classes and Clans

Ramaoide (elite members of the tribe)

Eilu Clan

> Great Head Chief Ekriaro - (grandfather - remained on island home)

First settlers on Volcanic Island

> Erangue (father)   Emenear (mother)
> Ekewane (girl 12)   Enara (boy 8)
> Equi (4)
> Daboi (baby boy-deceased)
> Gaida (uncle)   Erianga   (aunt)
> Eiru (girl 12 cousin)

Enename (middle class)

Iwa Clan

> Ramanmada (father) Enemame (mother)
> Ioopu (boy 16)   Emet (girl 14)
>
> Gope   (boy 16 Ioopu's friend)
> Ludi (girl 14 Emet's cousin and friend)

Sitio (lower class members of the tribe -slave like position)

Kalab Clan

Roqua (father)   Gorube (mother)
Emmar (boy 16)